THE
QUESTION
MARK

THE HOGARTH PRESS

52 Tavistock Square, London W.C.1.

Telephone: Museum 3488.

28 September, 1925

Miss M.Jaeger,
Honeywell Mount
Barnsley

Dear Madam,

      We have read your book "The Question Mark" with great in-
terest and should much like to publish it. We would offer to pay you
a royalty of 10% on the first 2000 copies sold, then 15% up to
4000, and 20% after 4000. Although we like the book very much,
it is, as you say,off the usual lines, and we feel that we are taking
the risk of there being very small sales; under these circumstances,
we must stipulate that royalties are not payable unless 500 copies
of the book are sold.

      If you agree to these terms, we would bring out the book during
the next spring season.

                Yours faithfully

                Leonard Woolf

THE
QUESTION
MARK

Muriel Jaeger

with an introduction by
DR MO MOULTON

This edition published 2019 by
The British Library
96 Euston Road
London NW1 2DB

Originally published in 1926 by The Hogarth Press

Cataloguing in Publication Data
A catalogue record for this book is available from the British Library

ISBN 978 0 7123 5298 7
e-ISBN 978 0 7123 6475 1

The frontispiece shows the letter from Leonard Woolf to 'Miss M.
Jaeger', confirming acceptance of *The Question Mark* for publication.
Reproduced with the permission of the Estate of Muriel Jaeger.

The photograph of Muriel Jaeger on page 6 of this edition is also
reproduced with the permission of the Estate of Muriel Jaeger.

Front cover illustration 'La Tour Noire. – Versant d'Argentières.' by
A.-C. Coppier. Originally published in *L'Illustration*, 3rd October 1925.

Typeset by Tetragon, London
Printed in England by CPI Group (UK) Ltd, Croydon, CR0 4YY

CONTENTS

INTRODUCTION

With the publication of her first novel, *The Question Mark*, in 1926, Muriel Jaeger helped to inaugurate a new genre: the modern dystopia. As she explains in her own introduction to the novel, she had grown tired of socialist utopian novels that imagined perfect people in a perfect future world. Instead, she wanted to know what happened to real people who had solved some of the twentieth century's most pressing problems—such as hunger, war, and the constant pressure of earning a living in a capitalist economy. *The Question Mark* takes a functioning socialist system as a given, adds some impressive technological advances made over two centuries, and asks: what next? What new dilemmas will people encounter or create, and how should we think about addressing them?

Although the novel is arguably more successful as an exploration of ideas than as work of narrative fiction, it is nonetheless quietly compelling as well as surprisingly enigmatic. Its hero, Guy Martin, finds himself transported from his dull life as a clerk in 1920s London to a pastoral, socialist twenty-second century. Like many such time-travelling protagonists, he becomes our guide to this new world as he slowly uncovers its triumphs and its fatal flaws. Various characters expound on their society for him, illuminating not only how it functions but also how they, as real people, fit into it.

In a particularly striking scene, Ena Wayland, the twenty-year-old daughter of the family with whom Martin is living, explains the "power-box" to Martin. This is a device the size of a cigarette case that has become a necessary appendage to life in the twenty-second century. (Though it is meant for the generation of power rather than for purposes of communication, the parallels with modern smartphones are worth pondering.) Like any utopian protagonist, Guy is intrigued by the device, and his questions to Ena expand our understanding of the economic and technical realities of this imagined future world. But Ena is a poor teacher: she doesn't really understand how the power-box works, and her dialogue is liberally sprinkled with the latest twenty-second-century slang. Far more vivid than the details of the power-box are her emotional reactions—her disdain at Guy's ignorance, her "delight in her superior knowledge," and her impatience with his technical questions. That emphasis is no accident. Power genera-tion has been more or less solved, but questions about knowledge, access to learning, and the balance between emotion and intellect haunt this apparently idyllic future.

The scene neatly confounds our expectations. Rather than being a passive representative of her society whose personality serves to add colour and interest to a technical explanation, Ena is in fact the whole point. Slyly, Jaeger invites us to see Ena as a 'silly young girl' likely to serve as nothing more than a potential love interest; then, she reveals that Ena's slang, her enthusiasms and her outbursts, are actually the novel's central device for laying bare the challenges facing this world.

Muriel Jaeger wrote *The Question Mark* aged around thirty, at a moment when she was struggling to make an independent life for herself. She was ideally placed to write the novel, not least because she would have had the experience of being seen as a silly young girl, albeit one who was able to take advantage of the dramatic increase in opportunities for higher education for women. She was born in the Yorkshire town of Barnsley in 1892, the daughter of John and Frances Jagger (the family would later change the spelling of its name). Her father was an auctioneer and estate agent; the family was sufficiently well-off to have a single live-in domestic servant. Muriel attended the Sheffield High School, an independent school for girls. From there, she won a Clothworkers' Scholarship worth £50 a year for three years to attend Somerville College, a women's college at Oxford University.

Jaeger entered Somerville in 1912. At that time, Oxford did not award degrees to women, though they were allowed to reside at women's colleges (technically still women's societies), to attend lectures, and to sit examinations. The principal of Somerville, Emily Penrose, required her students to take the examinations that would, in principle, qualify them for a degree; so Jaeger undertook a course of study in English.

At Somerville, Jaeger soon fell in with a group of literary-minded young women. They began meeting regularly, to share their writing and offer criticism; their most famous member, the future detective novelist Dorothy L. Sayers, dubbed them "The Mutual Admiration Society" before anyone else could call them that. Jaeger, too, got a new name: her friends would call her "Jim", following the fashion for masculine nicknames. In her schoolwork, her tutors found her to be "cautious and critical." She was more free-wheeling in the context of the Mutual Admiration Society, where she shared a "psychic story" in November 1913, a hint of her future preoccupations with psychology and mental phenomena. A few months later, she invited her friends to a 'ghost party', even going to the lengths of arranging for a 'ghost' to appear in the midst of it—actually another student, dressed in black lace and luminous paint.

Jaeger's studies at Somerville were interrupted several times because of illness, and she finished in 1916 with second-class honours in English. She would receive her actual degree as part of the first cohort of women granted them in 1920. Although many of her contemporaries went on to teaching or nursing, Jaeger instead moved to London and undertook work with government ministries. Her statistical work at the Ministry of Food exposed her to the starvation occurring in Germany and Austria, a useful context for understanding *The Question Mark*'s emphasis on the twenty-second century society's success in ensuring that all people had sufficient food.

After the war ended, Jaeger remained in London and began to try to make her way in the literary world. She and Sayers remained close—she visited Sayers in Oxford and later in France, and the two young women considered sharing a flat in London, though they never managed to do so. Jaeger began drafting a novel, a nostalgic story of university-educated women at the start of their careers featuring lightly-fictionalised versions of herself and of Sayers. It was not uncommon for a young person in Jaeger's position to publish a first novel about undergraduate life. Both Vera Brittain and Doreen Wallace, who were at Somerville around the same time, did so, with Brittain's *The Dark Tide* coming out in 1923 and Wallace's *A Little Learning* in 1931.

Although Jaeger drafted several versions of her Oxford novel, it was never published. She does, however, capture the flavour of her postwar London life in *The Question Mark*. Guy Martin's twentieth century life revolves around his efforts to find something more meaningful than his dull office job. He takes some evening classes, and he joins the Socialist Club, where, in Jaeger's dry, sarcastic, recounting, he makes friends with "educated, cultured young people, full of enthusiasm for social equality, and eager to show their indifference to class prejudice by making friends with bank clerks, or even with labourers, if such could be found." Here, she skewers the left wing members of her own class, who perform their open-mindedness rather unconvincingly.

Martin continues his "restless search for mental opiates" by attending "Theosophist lectures and services." This is a reference to Theosophy, a movement that began in the late nineteenth century and attracted many progressive-minded people with its emphasis on equality of people and world religions and its attractive blend of philosophy and mysticism, which would go on to inform New Age religions and movements.

All of this reflects Jaeger's own world in London in the early 1920s. She and Sayers attended a spiritualist meeting together, apparently fascinated by the spectacle of a minister whose sermons were delivered under the control of an unseen spirit. Through her work at the feminist periodical *Time & Tide*, Jaeger would have been in touch with the most advanced debates about feminism and social problems as well.

But she gave Martin something that she lacked: a steady job. Jaeger struggled to stay employed in the London literary scene. She earned a diploma in journalism from the University of London in 1920 and considered emigrating to Australia to work as a journalist there. Instead, she worked briefly for *Time & Tide* and for *Vogue*, but ill health and a tendency (in Sayers's view) to quarrel with her employers and to see menial work as beneath her prevented her staying any place for very long. Jaeger was somewhat hapless, too, landing back home with an infected finger in 1921 and scraping her leg on a bus in 1922. By that summer, she was worried that her family would stop helping her make ends meet in London, and indeed, she returned to Yorkshire that autumn.

At some point during this difficult, disorienting time, Jaeger wrote *The Question Mark*. In September 1925, the manuscript was accepted for publication by Hogarth Press, the independent project of Virginia and Leonard Woolf. In his letter to Jaeger, still at home in Barnsley, Leonard stipulated that no royalties would be paid unless they sold more than 500 copies: "Although we like the book very much, it is, as you say, off the usual lines," he explained.

The Question Mark came out in 1926. It was 'off the usual lines' in that it did not fit any of the genres then dominating the market for fiction; perhaps, too, the focus on science and socialism seemed surprising coming from a young, female, first-time author. But in its re-invention of utopian futurist literature, it spoke directly to the concerns of the moment. Eight years after the end of World War I, the world had grown impatient with the optimistic narratives of technological progress that animated the utopian fiction of the turn of the century.

In *The Question Mark*, Jaeger is reacting, specifically, to the utopian fiction of William Morris, Edward Bellamy, and H. G. Wells. As literary scholar Susan Stratton points out, *The Question Mark* alludes directly both to Bellamy's *Looking Backward* (1888) and to H. G. Wells' *The Time Machine* (1895). The premise—a protagonist arrives in the future through the means of a doctor whose family he joins—echoes Bellamy, while the slow revelation of unintended consequences parallels *The Time Machine*. The references to Bellamy and Wells are overt: indeed, Stratton even suggests that Ena's name is a combination of the names of the young female characters in the two earlier books—Edith and Weena.

Like Wells, Jaeger imagines that radical social change has led to the development of two distinct groups within humanity. Jaeger's writing, here, is influenced by the then-popular pseudo-science of eugenics, which argued that selective breeding could improve the overall health and intelligence of human beings. Such arguments were used to enforce racist hierarchies in the era; apart from a brief suggestion that left-wing intellectuals in the twentieth century were Jewish, Jaeger is less interested in this than in the possibility that human beings could evolve in such a way that their capacities either for intellectual inquiry or for emotion would predominate. In her novel, she thus creates a world divided between 'intellectuals' and 'normals'.

Such a division gives Jaeger an opportunity to criticise one of the dominant features of the early twentieth century world: the rise of mass communication, founded on rising literacy rates, increased access to leisure, and new media including radio and cinema. In *The Question Mark*, Jaeger begins to grapple with issues that would preoccupy her throughout her career: how could liberty be balanced with the need for an orderly society, given that people make foolish choices? How might education address the dangers of mass media, which threatens to manipulate people through the means of advertising, populist politics, and religious fads?

In addressing these issues through the means of speculative fiction, Jaeger was at the forefront of a wave of dystopian writing in the interwar decades. Indeed, Brian Stableford has argued that *The Question Mark* opened up lines of inquiry and criticism that would be pursued by others, most famously Aldous Huxley in his classic 1932 dystopian novel, *Brave New World*. Huxley, like Jaeger, is critical of mass culture, advertising, and the infantilisation of people into endlessly greedy consumers. And he, like Jaeger, asks whether apparent liberation can turn out to be nothing more than another trap. Stratton, meanwhile, argues that *The Question Mark* prefigures the "critical utopia" tradition in American science fiction writing of the 1960s.

Yet it would be reductive to see *The Question Mark* as merely a precursor to *Brave New World*. Such a view overlooks the originality of the novel's rewriting of Wells and Bellamy. As Chris Ferns has pointed out, dystopian classics such as Huxley's *Brave New World*, George Orwell's *Nineteen Eighty-Four* (1949), and Yevgeny Zamyatin's *We* (1924) remain trapped in the logic of the utopian fiction they are reacting to. Their rebels idealise the past (the reader's present), often praising, in particular, its regressive gender politics. Ferns sees all three of these novels ending with "the defeat of the rebellious male, the triumph of paternal authority, and the incidental destruction" of the female love-interest. They thus remain wedded to the all-consuming social control that typifies utopian literature and to the gender hierarchies that are common to the genre as well.

The Question Mark is very different and might even be seen as a precursor to the work of Margaret Atwood, which Ferns sees as breaking these generic conventions. Jaeger's book does not have the explicit feminist content of Atwood's novels. But, like *The Handmaid's Tale* (1985), it allows for the importance of subjective experience—the internal mental space that, unlike in *Nineteen Eighty-Four*, cannot be taken over by any external system, however coercive or invasive. Significantly, it even allows for the possibility that a young woman defined by the system as non-intellectual could experience that independent mental space, and could be a suffering, and indeed tragic, subject, instead of a mere plot device.

While formally echoing Wells and Bellamy, Jaeger's fiction also transcends their limitations in ways that other interwar writers did not. True to its title, the novel refuses to offer its readers a simple answer. *The Question Mark* ends with neither a tragedy nor a triumph, but a complex moment that leaves us to our own work of reflection and judgment.

DR MO MOULTON

SENIOR LECTURER, HISTORY DEPARTMENT

UNIVERSITY OF BIRMINGHAM

Further Reading

Chris Ferns, *Narrating Utopia: Ideology, Gender, Form in Utopian Literature* (Liverpool: Liverpool University Press, 1999)

Susan J. Leonardi, *Dangerous by Degrees: Women at Oxford and the Somerville College Novelists* (New Brunswick: Rutgers University Press, 1989)

Mo Moulton, *The Mutual Admiration Society: How Dorothy L. Sayers and Her Oxford Circle Remade the World for Women* (London: Little, Brown, 2019)

Elizabeth J. Morse, "Jaeger, Muriel," *Oxford Dictionary of National Biography* (23 Sept. 2004)

Brian Stableford, *Scientific Romance in Britain 1890-1950* (London: Fourth Estate, 1985)

Susan Stratton, "Muriel Jaeger's 'The Question Mark', a Response to Bellamy and Wells," *Foundation* 29 (Fall 2000)

THE
QUESTION
MARK

"When once we have got the economic sphere of social action reasonably organised on functional lines, we shall be free to forget about it most of the time, and to interest ourselves in other matters."   —G. D. H. COLE in *Social Theory*.

"Even if all education were free up to the highest, young people, unless they were radically transformed by the Anarchist régime, would not want more than a certain amount of it."

—BERTRAND RUSSELL in *Roads to Freedom*.

"As for love nowadays, one of our authors says that the vacuum left in the minds of men and women by the absence of care for one's livelihood has been entirely taken up by the tender passion."   —BELLAMY'S *Looking Backward*.

AUTHOR'S INTRODUCTION

It is a question of these Utopias. They become more and more numerous and more and more insistent. They assume a more and more practical, almost, one may say, a painful interest. For, while Plato and Bacon and Sir Thomas More never had, after all, to consider that their ideal societies might actually happen, or, at least, try to happen, we nowadays have to consider precisely that possibility. It appears every day more probable that the Socialist experiment will be tried, not wildly haphazard as in Russia, nor in the small half-playful model communities of the past, but soberly, on a large scale, by highly civilised nations, and with all the resources of civilisation.

And no one can say that we have not looked before we leaped. Many of our wise men have spent their lives looking and telling us what they saw. Some of them have told us in dry theoretic treatises, working out the minutest practical details; others (better known) have described the actual life of that future society to us in brightly coloured romances, as circumstantiated as a novel of Scott's about the past, and having the added advantage that no one can contradict them.

The Socialist answer is, in fact, the only plausible answer yet proposed to that terrible riddle embodied in Mr. Max Beerbohm's cartoon, in which the twisted, harrowed figure of the twentieth-century man gazes at the question mark which caricatures him and which represents his vision of his future.

I must confess at once that up to a certain point I find this answer convincing. Having listened to what they say, economists and romancers, and having observed the world around me according to my opportunities, I have been brought to the belief that it would be physically possible so to organise production and distribution that present social inequalities should disappear, and that at the same time there should be a great, though gradual, increase in general prosperity. Nor do I imagine it impossible to human nature that such a society should be established and maintained. It is, of course, an historical fact that such a society was established and maintained in the Peru of the sixteenth century—a civilisation finally destroyed by the accident of the horses and guns of the invading Spaniards, yet so exquisitely adjusted that, years after the wrecking of the central government, one province automatically supplied the needs of its famine-stricken neighbour. The fact that this co-operative state existed has always seemed to me a sufficient answer to those who say that a co-operative state could not exist—even though, to be sure, the participants were only Indians, and lived some time ago and a long way off.

Apart from this, I cannot feel that there is any great rashness in supposing that Europeans, who have lived successively under the régimes of the Roman Empire, Feudalism, and the comparatively recent mushroom growth of Competitive Industrialism, will be able also to live under the régime of modern Socialism.

In the imaginary Jerusalem, therefore, which prophets have built for me in England's green and pleasant land, Socialism is established; it succeeds; it works well. It is not, of course, the rigid State Socialism of the earlier nineteenth-century thinkers, but the freer, more adaptable Socialism of to-day, fertilised by the ideals of Anarchism and Syndicalism, chastened by the lessons of the Russian experiment—the Socialism, in fact, now definitely projected by our advanced politicians. It has led to prosperity and to a partial release from Adam's curse of toil. In short, I accept the Bellamy-Morris-Wells world in all essentials—with one exception; I do not and cannot accept its inhabitants. At this point my effort to realise Utopia fails. With the best will in the world, I have found myself quite unable to believe in these wise, virtuous, gentle, artistic people. They do not seem to have any relation to humanity as I know it—even by the most distant descent; they suggest, rather, Special Creation.

I have discovered also that I am not alone in this inability. Other people also have found the Utopians more difficult to swallow than the Utopias. Conditions, no doubt, would modify human nature as they always do; but would they, could they, modify it quite like that? We cannot see it. Very regretfully we are driven to wonder whether some of our philosophers have not here leapt a chasm from what they might deduce to what they would wish. And it seems that others of them, coming to the verge of discovery, have delicately stepped away again, leaving this last and most portentous problem of Utopia still shrouded in veils of mystery. None the less, such vague hints as are quoted on the front page of this book have, to my mind, more vitality in them than all the tall, sun-warmed, intelligently voluble athletes to whom we have been so frequently introduced.

It appeared that the only hope was to go and see for one's self; and so I was led into the adventure which is represented by this book. My Utopia was given; but I would people it for myself, or, rather, let it people itself for me. Social and economic conditions could be taken for granted; they have been exhaustively described by our predecessors in Utopia, and all who take any interest in that region are already familiar with them. The factors of my problem are these conditions and human nature as we know it. I invited them to combine in my book and to come to life. How they have responded to the invitation is for the reader to judge.

The game is started in the old accepted manner. My hero, the twentieth-century man, whom we need for our interpretative chorus, is transferred to the England of the future, when the turmoil of the change is over, the Socialist régime is working prosperously, and wealth and leisure have become as common as they now are rare. This supernormal transference is the one marvel that the rules of my game will allow me, the key marvel on which the rest depends. Otherwise there must be no romantic scientific miracles to obscure the issue, except such as are already so plainly foreshadowed as to be almost certainties. Indeed, they are unnecessary. For, if we had, even now, the time and the capital and the concord and the common sense to put in the latest machinery—in the widest sense—is there any doubt that we should find ourselves in a world sufficiently transformed?

But when I have got my hero thus with all due ceremony into the future, he must take what comes. The Utopians will be there to welcome him, the few usual figures who always receive such visitors with the calm courtesy of mediæval damsels receiving a knight as he drops on the magic carpet into their castle courtyard. But further I refuse to coerce them. They must develop their own natures like everyone else. If they walk away with my story in the meantime, I shall not grumble. It will at any rate be a sign of life.

It is that life that will be lived in those Nowheres—Nowheres perhaps about to become Somewheres; about, perhaps, to become

HERE—that I am in search of. And it is those who share my curiosity about this Question Mark whom I invite also to share my adventure, hoping that the clumsiness of the guide may be forgiven in the interest of the quest.

MURIEL JAEGER

CHAPTER I

THE HERO

I

I CALLED FOR A HERO—ONE WHO SHOULD BE TYPICAL OF THE England of 1925—and there appeared gradually developing out of the obscurity a very unheroic little figure, Guy Martin, shoving and dodging his way along the Strand on a rainy autumn evening. He comes in an aura of distress and rebellion, but rebellion shot with futility—a personality as little glamorous as one could well imagine. Yet, perhaps, he will become more heroic as we go on. Certainly, if there is any truth in the modern view that experience ennobles, he is to have his chance.

His distress is, at first sight, paradoxical, for it was due to the fact that he had not lost his job at the London and Imperial Bank that afternoon. It was due, however, to the fact that he had not had the courage to lose it. For days past he had been firmly resolved that the next time Burrows, the manager of the branch, broke out into his bullying snarl to him, Guy—he, Guy—would give Burrows as good as he got and devil might take the consequences. But this afternoon the awaited outbreak had occurred, and the habit of sub-ordination had prevailed after all. Instinctively, Guy had stammered apologetically under the torrent of curt, contemptuous sentences, and, before he could recover his wits sufficiently to compose a deliberate retort, Burrows had turned away with a final snap:

"The next time this happens, you'll go, Martin, and that's all about it."

Guy had put away his books and got his hat and coat, almost crying with suppressed rage, and had lashed out viciously at a fellow-clerk who attempted some jocular commiseration. Humiliation to a rebellious nature often works greater nervous havoc than much greater practical misfortunes. And Guy never could, like the rest of them, take Burrows' explosions with Cockney philosophy, as if they were some natural catastrophe like a thunderstorm, nor console himself with vulgar jokes and smoke-room stories about him behind his back. It comforted immensely Tomlinson, for instance, the youth whose sympathy had just been vainly offered, to represent Burrows as miserably henpecked by a diminutive wife in his Hampstead flat, and to draw secret schoolboy caricatures of the henpecking process. But, for Guy, more semblance of reality in his retaliations was necessary.

He was not very popular with his fellow-workers, nor, in truth, very popular anywhere, for he thought a great deal about his dignity and his self-respect, and such preoccupations do not make for popularity. He had found, however, some solace in wearing a red tie and belonging to a Socialist club. Here he could mix in a somewhat artificial equality with people of all classes, and, in constantly attacking and hearing attacked the existing organisation of society, could "get back" on Burrows and his kind in a manner which, seeming to have some potentiality of ultimate realisation, was more satisfying to him than whisperings and caricatures.

There was nothing that Guy would have liked less than to be called typical; and yet, as he struggles through the obstacle race of the Strand at the time of closing offices, he represents for us the England of the early twentieth century. He was discontented; he was a clerk; and he worked in a bank—one of the great central-power stations which fed that infinitely complicated, self-evolved machinery of credit and commerce which sustained, bewildered, and terrorised twentieth-century society. He had, moreover, the appearance typical of many lower-middle-class young Englishmen of the time—a slim physique, a fairish and open face, pale with indoor living, yet not entirely unprepossessing, blue eyes, and an indeterminate nose and chin. In fact, he looked just like everyone else, and, in addition, his name was Martin. For some obscure reason, every other person in the great clerking class of that time seems to have been called Martin. One was almost as certain to hit the mark in addressing a young man at a desk, or a young woman at a typewriter, as Mister, or Miss, Martin, as in calling an Irish peasant "Pat."

But this particular young Mr. Martin had other associations also, and these were symbolised in his first name, "Guy." For his mother's grandmother had been the daughter of a baronet, and Mrs Martin had not been able to forget this fact when her son had been born at the little village store down in Kent. And so she had called him "Guy"—a very usual name for the descendants of baronets in the novelettes that she was accustomed to read behind the counter. Guy had come to resent his name bitterly as he grew up and, mixing with the world, learnt how many other people of his own class had succumbed to similar influences; so that the young men who went to Oxford were now, as often as not, Tom, Dick, or Harry, while those who waited on them were the Clarences, the Howards, and the Guys. But, not being highly self-analytical in temperament, he thought that his resentment was merely for his mother's snobbishness. Nothing was more certain than that he himself no longer had any respect for class distinctions.

The bitterness in which Guy grew to manhood was fundamentally due to the fact that he had been one of those cleverish children whose mental alertness disappears at adolescence. His brains had carried him as far as a scholarship at the Grammar school in the neighbouring town, but no further. After that achievement, he had become slack. He remained always vaguely ambitious, but immediate results had no longer seemed worth the effort of mental concentration necessary to attain them. He always meant to settle down to vigorous work at some future time, when, he told himself, he would easily make up the lost ground, but the commencement of the effort was always postponed. After a time, the masters at the school had lost patience and ceased to bother about him, and when he had barely scraped through his matriculation examination, they had not considered it worth while to coach him for a university scholarship. His mother was told accordingly that the scholarship he held at the school could no longer be renewed, and at seventeen he was thrown back on the family resources.

Guy, himself, covered up the consciousness of his failure with the conviction that they had taken no pains with him, because his mother was only a small shopkeeper. And, no doubt, the son of a factory-owner would have received more attention.

Guy's fate, therefore, had been the bank, and a constant grudge against society from the age of seventeen. The only mitigation was that he was placed at a London branch, where his uncle (also a member of the clan of Martins) was already working. His father had died of consumption long before. His mother still managed the diminishing business of the little village shop, as it struggled hopelessly against the newly opened branch of a co-operative society. She wrote brief, illiterate, rambling letters to Guy, hinting always at the end that she was short of money and that she wished he would come home—two incompatible desires that he never answered in words. He sent her, however, a pound a week, living in a Bermondsey slum in order to do so, and went down to her for his two weeks' holiday in the summer. He had never anywhere else to go.

But he had never got used to his own commonplaceness. The childhood impression of his exceptional quality, augmented by foolishly admiring elders, had persisted. Such impressions, early received and closely entwined with self-love, do not die easily. He always believed that he could have done great things (the nature of which remained unspecified) if he had only been given his chance.

Guy Martin had become of military age during the last year of the European War of 1914–18, and had left the bank for a short period of training. This had not, however, left him with that feeling of comradeship for the upper classes of which so much was said at the time. His secret intention had been never to return to the bank afterwards, but peace and demobilisation caught him with alternative plans unmade, and inexorable circumstances forced on him the conviction that he was exceptionally fortunate in having a job worth £3, 10s. a week to go back to. Sheer want of practical initiative finally drove him back before it was too late.

In his early twenties which followed, intellectual curiosity revived in him to some extent—enough, that is, for him to begin several Polytechnic evening courses and drop them half-way through, and to attend odd meetings and lectures. He also ran through a fair number of the little series volumes which catered for the peculiar twentieth-century blend of desire for knowledge and mental laziness, by condensing every art and science into a few pages of simple language and clear type. Finally, he had joined the Socialist Club.

There, at last, he had made friends, the kind of friends to whose friendship he had always felt himself entitled—educated, cultured young people, full of enthusiasm for social equality, and eager to show their indifference to class prejudice by making friends with bank clerks, or even with labourers, if such could be found. At times, during this last year or two, he had been almost happy with the satisfaction of avowed and shared discontent. He might have been happy altogether, if his ear had not caught now and again the sound of his own Cockney vowels—of which, in spite of hours of ridiculous and humiliating practice, difficult to explain away to himself, he could never completely rid himself; or if he had not been perpetually conscious of the contrast between his own stiffly carried body and genteel clothes, and the loosely built, carelessly dressed, classless young fellows who lounged and harangued on the Club hearth-rugs. At times he almost hated them; and the fact that many of them had thin, darkish, intelligent faces, often with some slight prominence of the nose, perhaps added a flavour of unperceived racial antipathy to his hatred.

These things—his disabilities—had troubled him more since he had met Marjorie Cannon at the Club. In the end they had loomed so large that he had posted to Marjorie that foolish, desperate letter which he had been alternately regretting and rejoicing in all day, and the anxiety about which underlay his present self-loathing.

For Marjorie had been nice to him, but never quite nice enough. They had played so hard that there was no gulf between them, that, at times, even in the depths of his heart, Guy had almost been able to disbelieve in its existence. And yet he had never been able to advance beyond a certain point with her. Something intangible, but insuperable, had always stopped him on the verge of real intimacy, some woman's cobweb that was like a steel net when one got caught in it. Not that it was possible to suspect Marjorie of insincerity—she was of the type that radiates sincerity. She was tall, very young, with a bobbed mop of golden-brown hair, the daughter of a well-known Church of England preacher. She herself had been recently converted to Socialism and Agnosticism, and was putting into their propaganda all her father's intensity. And now, after months of a charming and sympathetic friendliness, she had begun to look preoccupied, to seem older and remoter, and to come less and less to the Club. At last, after a fortnight without a glimpse of her, Guy had reached the point of exasperation, and had written.

It was for this reason that he could not, that night, take refuge at the Club, as was his custom when affairs at the bank had provoked him beyond endurance. He could not go there again until he had her answer. It occurred to him now that there was a chance that this answer might be already delivered at his lodgings. Marjorie always replied to letters promptly. He quickened his step, cannoning into men and women who were trying to progress in the opposite direction... By God! If she had not failed him, what a man he could become...

Childishly vague visions of glory hovered in his brain—wonderful achievements for the Cause, fierce raids against the oppressors. With her, he could do anything. It would take more than a Burrows to cow him then! He half-consciously began to attribute his failure of the afternoon to his state of uncertainty. No one could be expected to have all his wits about him under such circumstances. He hastened his pace again, plunged recklessly across Wellington Street traffic, and, determined to spend an ill-spared penny in reaching his destination more quickly, hurled himself into a bus-scrum at the pavement edge.

Using his weight, he ploughed apart a crowd of squealing, chattering women, and with a spring got on to the steps. He climbed to the top, the last man on, with lingering sensations of pointed shoes trodden underfoot, elbowed masses of soft bodies, and the smart of a hatpin-scratch on his cheek.

The rain fell, soft, penetrating, and chilling. He was beginning to shiver before he dropped off the bus beyond Waterloo. He turned up a side-street into a quiet square, a relic of days when the district had been inhabited by a prosperous population, and inserted his latch-key in the door of a shabby-genteel house, one of whose attics was his home. The letter, addressed in Marjorie's delicate handwriting, was lying on the hall table.

At the sight of it, Guy's briskness suddenly left him. His heart stopped, then began to race. He found himself trembling so violently that his teeth began to chatter. He stumbled to the table and picked up the letter, looking at it with terror, and began shakily, half-crouching, to climb the long staircases up to his room. He was exhausted when he got there, and sat shivering in the arm-chair for a few moments before he could open the envelope.

The kind, suave, fluent phrases seemed to go over him like warm waves. He could not immediately gather the sense.

"You are so right and so sound, always; you understand so well. You and I have thought enough to be able to face it out. There is a difference, as you say. Of course, there ought not to be, but, as things are, for our generation, it is and must be so. And one has only this one life—at least, so far as we know."

Gently turned, diabolically convincing, the bitter assertions of his own letter came back upon him.

"Guy, dear, if you and I lived in the same house, we should get on each other's nerves in a thousand little ways. We both know it, so why not be brave and say so? You are brave, I know. The things are little, but they would be there all the time. And for the big moments—the moments when one can afford to be big—we can be such good friends. And we can work so hard—each in our own environment—for the people who are to come after, so that, for them, the difference shall never be there… You will go on being friends, won't you, Guy? I don't know of anything I have ever valued more than your friendship. That two people like us can meet sometimes and talk and understand each other as we do, I think is the most wonderful and the most promising thing…"

Then, just at the end: "I've met such an interesting man lately— and at one of those dinner parties of Mother's that I've always hated so much! It is a Mr. Warren, one of the new progressive Conservatives. You must go and hear him speak some time. Of course, he does not altogether agree with us, but he goes quite a long way, and some of his ideas are well worth considering…"

II

Thus the affair began with shock and psychological disaster. It was when Guy returned to full self-consciousness again that the great temptation occurred.

He had found himself hurrying in the darkness along a narrow riverside street. For he was one of those who rush into physical exertion in moments of mental stress, driven by old blind instinct to seek a remedy for the torments of the soul, just as his primitive ancestors had fought or fled from their material enemies.

The drizzling rain was falling cool on his cheek. His shoddy overcoat was drenched and his limbs were aching—he knew that he had been walking for hours. But the acuteness of his suffering was over for the moment. He felt his brain poised and clear with the deceptive lucidity which comes from the combination of fasting and nervous strain. He had the impression of balancing on a tight-rope—at present, he stood clear and disinterested, aloof, but knowing that the slightest disturbance of equilibrium might plunge him back into the horror of realisation. Instinctively, he turned homeward, savouring, almost enjoying, his sense of irresponsibility.

And then the temptation came—not a physical temptation; he was mentally too detached by slight fever for suicide to occur to him—but one of those psychical temptations which probably most people have experienced, but of which few will speak. This one was, perhaps, constitutional to Guy.

It had begun in boyhood, in a not uncommon mental trick which he would play when people had vexed him, and he had no means of redress. It consisted in a self-suggested conviction that they did not actually exist, that, in fact, the whole universe outside himself had no reality, but occurred only as part of his consciousness—was, in the childish phrase, his dream. For this idea is, indeed, not only a philosophic theory, but a psychological state. In this way, the boy Guy Martin would spiritually annihilate his enemies and find comfort.

The trick had left him as he grew older, but a circumstance of late years had brought it back. In his restless search for mental opiates, he had for a time attended Theosophist lectures and services, and, under this stimulus, the tendency had reasserted itself. He had realised its connection with the trance state so often described and discussed at the meetings and in the books that were given to him. Once, when alone in his room, he had attempted it, seeking to isolate and draw in his mind on itself, letting the outside world drop away, piece by piece, image by image, until nothing was left but the absolute self. And he had felt the process actually beginning; the objects around him had receded, become blurred; his consciousness had gathered in on itself. He had been aware that the final severance was approaching when terror had struck him suddenly, terror of the Unknown into which he was regressing, a panic-stricken home sickness for the familiar world of sense. For a moment his soul had gasped and floundered like a swimmer too long under water; then, with a dislocating effort, he had moved his arm, and, with the movement, come up to life again.

This experience had scared him. Since that day he had shunned the temptation to begin the withdrawal, as a man with a weak head will shun the high window from which he is impelled to pitch himself. He had resisted it even though, now and then, in vacant, solitary moments, it would come almost as irresistibly as the pull of the tongue to a hollow tooth. Lately, since the Club had given him a more sociable life, such moments had been rarer, and he had begun to forget. But now, as he walked through the damp night, the temptation was on him again, and this time the springs of his instinctive resistance were there no longer. The will-to-live had left him.

If Guy had met anyone, no doubt, the moment would have passed him by. He would have been forced to come back, to feel human contact, to revive his human sense of proportion. But he met no one. It was after midnight, and the house was dark and silent. He slipped quietly up to his room.

He switched on the light and lay down on his bed, fixing his eyes upon the glaring bulb. Almost at once his body became rigid and his breath began to come more and more slowly. The objects

in the room—the patchy ceiling and the peeling walls; the little
shoddy washstand; the line of clothes on hooks unconcealed by
a half-drawn, dirty curtain; the deal table on which lay the white
square of Marjorie's letter—were all within his field of vision; but
they were receding slowly under the force of his inward concentration. They were soon no longer solid objects, but flat patches
of light and shade; they began to blur and run into each other.
The tick of the alarm clock on the mantelpiece was passing into
a vague impression of a continuous murmuring sound, dropping
more and more into the distance. He was no longer conscious of
the contact of the bed beneath him, but seemed to be floating,
unsupported, in space. Only the bright bulb of the electric light
remained, and that was spreading and approaching; it became a
diffuse glow which gradually enveloped him. Guy knew that the
supreme moment of abnegation was at hand, and terror snatched
at him again. But this time his will held firm. At last, that too passed
away, and he was alone.

CHAPTER II

THE PASSAGE

AGES OF SILENCE PASSED BY. GRADUALLY HE BECAME AWARE that he was no longer alone, and experience began again. The things that happened to him there in the gulf behind Time cannot be shown in words or symbols, since they have no relationship to sense impressions. And yet, when Guy turned at last and faced his own history, he represented the thing to himself in images, since in no other way can normal human thought occur or give itself expression. Yet he was conscious of the illusion even as he did so.

This translation into symbolism gave it to him as if he had been standing in some vast space in a semi-darkness that was like dusk when it is becoming night, or night when it is becoming dawn. Beside him lay, as on a raised bier, a long, straight figure swathed entirely in white wrappings, so that only the face remained exposed. Sometimes he thought that the eyes had been open, sometimes that they had been shut. The features were still, white, and rigid, and they were his own, perfected. He knew that the figure was, in some way, himself, even while he stood beside and gazed at it. And, at the same time, he knew that it was also a being infinitely more significant than himself, as if the intimate essence of a man should have meanings and affinities on which his composite personality had no bearing.

He knew further that the figure was not dead, although it lay in absolute passivity. It was suffering supremely. Its stillness expressed the perfect consummation of endurance.

For countless ages he watched beside it in the silence, without change or movement, his gaze held by the white placid face, his soul concentrated on the locked struggle of the forces of torture and endurance, perfectly balanced, holding each other motionless like two unconquerable wrestlers pressed together in an unending opposition.

And then that also passed away.

CHAPTER III

THE UNDISCOVERED COUNTRY

I

IT SEEMED TO GUY THAT HE WAS COMING OUT INTO THE LIGHT through a series of pillared stone porticoes each opening out into the next. Every slow step brought him a stage farther into a larger space and nearer to the sunshine gleaming ahead. At last he stepped out into the cool, fresh air, into a sea of light and space. And then the eyes of his body opened.

For a few seconds he looked upon the new world, for the duration of a few half-conscious, fleeting impressions—a feeling of spaciousness about him, a vision of a section of distant stone roof high above his head, arched like the porticoes of his dream, the sensation of lying at length upon a yielding pallet. Then there were hands moving about his body, and a face came suddenly across his vision, a queerly foreshortened face with bright grey eyes, which looked down into his with such potency that they seemed to expand, becoming slowly the whole universe. The movements slid down his arms from shoulder to wrist. Somewhere, far off, a voice was repeating tonelessly, hardly removed from the silence, "Sleep, sleep; you must sleep, sleep, sleep."

II

The next time Guy awakened naturally. He found himself in the little lighted room with its queer, flimsy-looking furniture, its knobs and switches, and its front wide to the sun, with no more surprise than if he had awakened in his dingy attic in Bentley Square. Already in his mind was the assurance that all that was over, that he was awakening to a new world and a new life, and that all these things were natural and necessary.

The assurance was connected with the man who moved about the room attending to his wants, now and then stopping merely to smile at him, sometimes feeding him with unfamiliar, but delicious drinks. He was a middle-aged man with a finely built, intelligent face, and bright grey eyes. His clothing was white and loose-fitting—a shirt and short trousers. He told Guy that his name was Wayland, and that he was a doctor. They talked very little at first; but Guy knew that somewhere, remotely, they had talked already; that the other knew all about him, and that it was through him that he had received this certainty that all was well with him. A world, no longer wretched, but full of interest and beauty, was waiting for him as soon as he should be ready to go out into it. All question as to how this had come to be was banished from his consciousness. At present he lay in a happy languor, more perfectly at peace than ever before in his life. It was as though he had lost his human forlornness, as if he were a man who had come into touch with a powerful, familiar, kindly god.

For that day he lay, hardly moving. Now and then the outside world would recede again and he would seem to be floating over a blue sea in mild, veiled sunshine, while light ideas came to him like little white sailing ships. Sometimes, afterwards, he would think that Dr. Wayland had talked to him again in those intervals, had asked him questions and told him things that he must know. For he understood more and more clearly that he would find the world different, strangely different, when he went out into it; and yet he was not afraid. It would not be utterly foreign to him; it would be the reality of what he had always craved.

III

The next day the outside world had become more definite. It was still dream-like, but it was nearer and clearer, like a dream that was slowly becoming true. Throughout the first weeks of Guy's life in the new age this gradual approach continued, as the magical haze resting on his brain cleared slowly.

That day he was allowed to stagger on unsteady limbs to the wide window space, which strangely and fascinatingly moved round with the sun, and to look out for a few moments on to a delicious summer landscape of green meadows and groves of darker green, through which would sometimes thrust itself the white shoulder of a house or cottage. In the near distance a river gleamed, a silver band appearing and disappearing among the trees.

"England. It's still England?" he murmured questioningly.

"Still England," Dr. Wayland beside him said quietly.

In a neighbouring field a glittering, smokeless machine was mowing grass at an astonishing rate, apparently quite unattended, moving up and down the broad rows and turning at the ends with a quaint military precision. He gave a little laugh of delight as he watched it, like a child seeing a mechanical toy set in motion for his pleasure.

"You'll see many things like that," said Dr. Wayland, following his glance.

For that time Guy was glad to get back on to the bed. But through the next days his strength began to return with a sweep that was like the swell of a breaker under the swimmer riding in upon it.

And, as his strength came back, the world expanded around him.

He knew the little room well by this time—which lever swung round the bath already filling with water; into which wall cupboard he must drop his garments every night that they might return to him smooth and spotless in the morning; how to manipulate the sliding shutters so that he could follow or exclude the sun all day long. Now it was time to go farther afield.

IV

He dressed that morning like Dr. Wayland, in a light white shirt and trousers, free for ever from the oppression of stiff collars. The Doctor watched him smilingly. He had hardly ever left him alone during these days of his convalescence, and Guy had seen no one else. He had been perfectly content that it should be so, but now he was beginning to wonder, to want to see farther, to go down and explore the strange paradise which he had overlooked from his window.

He stepped over to the mirror to shave, and for a moment his brain reeled. It was the first time since his awakening that he had looked closely at his own face. As he did so now, he received a staggering impact—a strong, though instantly fleeting, impression that the face that looked back at him was not his own. It was like a moment of mental dislocation, the vertigo of a faint or a heart attack, and his instinctive glance at Dr. Wayland, who was watching him with quiet eyes, instantly calmed him. He saw, as he looked again, that apart from a slight haggardness, the image in the glass was, after all, feature by feature, the Guy Martin that he knew, even to a tiny birth-mark on the left side of the neck. He half turned, smiling, to confide his alarm; but Dr. Wayland had begun to speak of other things, and the perturbation slipped easily from his mind.

The house seemed full of the June sunshine as they passed down through it. The square space, half-hall, half-lounge, into which they descended by the broad, shallow staircase, stretched with no narrowing into the stone terrace in front. Through open panels, as he passed down, Guy caught a glimpse of charmingly shaped rooms with divans and cushions and light chairs; a place made for pleasant living, yet deserted. There was no one about.

Dr. Wayland did not allow him to linger, but brought him out to a group of lounge chairs on the terrace and made him sit down. The house behind them, of a delicate cream-coloured substance which Guy could not identify, half wide through its many shutters to the air, looked as frail and dainty as a bird's eggshell lying in a wood.

Below them a flower-garden stretched down in the direction of the river. Guy's impression that he had never seen such a garden before was immediate, but it was some moments before he realised what was the secret of it—that the whole was a design in orange and purple against the green background. Flowers of luxuriant bloom in every shade of the chosen colours clustered around the masses of trees and bushes, sometimes in a graduated series of tints, sometimes in harmonious contrasts. Later, Guy discovered a blue garden of a celestial delicacy, and a flaming red and yellow one, and many other combinations, but he never became blunted to the half-magical effect of this union of scenic art with fresh living growth.

Dr. Wayland sat beside him, smoking for a few moments; then he rose, saying that he must visit his laboratory. His eyes dwelt thoughtfully on Guy as he spoke, and Guy felt the thrill of a promoted child as the other turned to walk away. He understood that to be left by himself marked a stage in his new life.

When the Doctor had actually gone the sense of adventure grew upon him until his body and soul seemed to quiver with expectancy, yet without any element of fear. An inner conviction of security remained with him.

The day was exquisitely fresh and calm. The morning coolness had not yet left the air, though the sun was growing in strength from moment to moment. And with every moment the colours of grass and trees and flowers seemed to change a little, becoming more intense, altering subtly their relations to one another. Now and then a light breeze, moving among the leaves, made a shimmering variation. It was an enchanting world. Guy became more and more conscious of his solitude in it. He lighted another cigarette from the case that Dr. Wayland had given to him that morning. He thought that it was a strangely quiet and spacious world as well as beautiful. It was barely conceivable that London slums had once covered this very spot, as the Doctor had told him. Now there was no one in sight.

He realised now what was the essence of his expectancy. It was the people of the new world whom he was waiting to see—the human beings who would give significance to all the beauty. The house had seemed empty as they passed through it. Yet he knew that it was a homestead, for Dr. Wayland had told him that he was married and that his wife had not wished to live in a community house.

He hoped venturously that someone would come while Dr. Wayland was away from him.

As if in answer to the wish, a girl ran out of the house impetuously and stopped short suddenly as she saw him. She retreated a little, gazing at him bright-eyed, half dodging round a pillar of the veranda like a shy child. She was bare-legged and wore a purple tunic with a silver girdle; a silver fillet kept a mass of fuzzy dark hair from falling over her eyes.

"I know who you are." She spoke after a moment with a curious mixture of childish shyness and audacity. "Father put me to sleep and told me. He is going to do the same to mother when she comes down. He's doing it so that we shouldn't be startled. But you don't look startling. You look just the same as anyone else... You're going to stay here, aren't you? Did you like coming?"

Guy began to answer, but she interrupted him at once.

"And I want madly"—she evidently used the word to intensify, as "awfully" had once been used—"I want madly to know what colour your power-box is going to be."

Guy laughed out. It was not what he had expected. He had contemplated vaguely some graceful, statuesque figure stepping like a pagan god or nymph out of that wonderful landscape to embody to him the humanity of the new world; not this quaint, bright little person clinging monkey-like round the post of the veranda.

"But what's that?" he asked as to a child. "I've heard of powder-boxes, but..."

"But it's the colour—the colour—I want to know." She came out from behind the pillar and ventured nearer in her vehemence. Her small face was in constant play; she emphasised her phrases with little ducks of the head at the person she was speaking to, shaking her mop of curls. "Tell me your favourite colour, Martin. Be quick!"

"Well, blue, I think," he said, smiling at her.

The little figure hurled itself at him, a mass of warm, fresh scentedness. He felt himself hugged violently, and moist lips pressed against his cheek.

"You darling! I said it would be. That's my favourite colour, too. But you mustn't have just the same shade or there will be mad muddles. I am always leaving mine about. Will you let me help you to choose yours? You must!"

Guy was still gasping from the embrace.

"You must forgive my daughter," Dr. Wayland's calm voice spoke just behind him. "She is a child yet. But you will have to grow up soon, Ena." He turned to her, frowning a little. "You are twenty, after all."

"Oh, father, as if it made any difference!" the girl pouted. "I am not going to be an intellectual, that is certain, so mother says I had better stay young as long as possible."

"Perhaps she is right." Dr. Wayland turned away with a slight sigh. "But don't embrace Martin." He smiled at Guy. "You will frighten him. He comes from a less demonstrative age than ours."

For a moment his hand rested on Guy's wrist; then, with a satisfied nod, he turned to go in again. Guy realised with a new confidence that he was deemed fit now to be left to his own resources. He looked back to the girl.

But her impulsiveness seemed to have been succeeded by a reaction of shyness. She was standing half-turned away, concentrated on the arrangement of a bunch of flowers at her waist. He could not think of her as being twenty years old, as her father had said. She seemed a much younger girl. But then it passed through his mind that these marvellous people of the new age would naturally have an extended childhood. He remembered a scrap of scientific information from one of those little series volumes, that the higher the type, the longer was the period of immaturity. That would account for her childishness.

"I wish you would tell me," he said gently, "what is a power-box?"

She turned with a little whirl, letting the flowers fall at random. Her eyebrows rose almost into her hair.

"You don't know? Really, you don't?" She laughed a little triumphantly. "I can show you one for the first time!... Look!"

She pulled from a pocket in her tunic a box of some metallic substance about the size of a cigarette case, painted a deep blue shade. As she touched a catch, the end swung open, letting out a short tube ending in a metal screw.

"You see?" She seemed to consider the article self-explanatory.

"But what do you do with that?" Guy demanded. The small object looked so lifeless and insignificant that its name, which had caught his imagination, seemed absurd.

"God! You are ignorant." Her delight in her superior knowledge was too naïve to annoy him. "Well, you fasten it to things, of course. Anything you want to make go."

"To make go?"

"Yes, an aerocycle, or a stereomovie, or a heater—anything. They all have places to screw it on."

Guy examined the little article with eager caution, while Ena laughed at him. He could not recognise the white, light metal, and she could tell him nothing but its name, which was one he did not know. She would not open the case for him.

"God!" (The exclamation seemed to have become as common as the French *Mon Dieu!*) "I don't understand the things," she said disdainfully. "You will have to ask a mechanic if you want to know all that."

"Does everyone have one?" Guy asked.

"Oh yes, of course. How do you suppose anyone could manage without? One couldn't go anywhere or do anything. Everyone who draws pay gets a refill every month along with his coupons, and no one could use all that if he went round and round the world without stopping. It is a pity father hasn't one to give you, but you see he has to supply Terry and me, as we are not working. Mother doesn't get more than enough for herself, because she did only part of her work-term. But John has several. He's coming here to-morrow to see you. He'll easily spare one for you."

Guy's mind stood still with wonder for a moment as he realised that what John was to give him so casually was what corresponded to a large slice of a man's income in the old times—certainly, it seemed, the means of travelling, of warming, lighting, and entertaining himself—most of the small conveniences of everyday life. He moved luxuriously in his chair, realising for the first time the magical comfort of wealth. The ideas which had passed into his consciousness in those dream-like interludes of the last days ranged orderly through his brain. He remembered that the days of economic stress were gone for ever. That terrible force which had kept half one's mind always astrain, compressed, in terror, like a half-dead rat pinched in a trap; the brutal, bullying force never to be quite forgotten even in life's most blessed moments—it was gone. It seemed to him that that was why the sky was so blue, the air so fresh, the flowers so brilliant; that was why one could laugh and talk freely and take everything with gay inconsequence, why the world had this fascinating fairy-tale aspect. By this time no one would starve even if he did nothing at all. Food was too plentiful and free as water. All the world was rich. It followed that no man could be forced or blackmailed by the ultimate threat. He would work for what he wanted beyond elementary necessities, but not under duress. Ena's casual remark had given all this reality. He sighed and moved his limbs as if chains had been knocked off them.

A release from the need of afterthought—nothing to do but to enjoy. He turned with renewed interest to his companion.

"Is John your brother?" he asked her.

"No, no," Ena laughed. "He's my cousin—he's a student; and you know what that means." She went on without giving him time to ask an explanation. "Terry is my brother. To tell you the truth," she had come to rest on a little table by his side, and leaned forward to him confidentially, "I think father would be glad if it were John instead... But we don't mind. It is a fine thing to belong to the family of a mountain racer."

"A mountain racer! What on earth is that?"

Ena laughed again at his ignorance. "How funny you don't even know that! A mountain racer—well, he's a mountain racer, you know. He races up mountains. Terry has won the English championship. They say he is the best English racer there has been for ten years."

"Do you mean to say that they race to see who can get up a mountain first?"

"Yes, of course. It takes two or three days generally. But they are having quite a short one, a day's climb, soon. It's an international one, in Switzerland, without guides. Mother and I mean to go.

It's the first time Terry has entered for an international race. You ought to come with us. It will be a sublime sight. Terry hardly got away last time on a fast aerocycle; they almost smothered him. He is training in the Tyrol now, so you won't see him until it is over."

Mountain racing! Guy remembered in the old days the Marathon races, the walks from London to Brighton. He had once seen the finish of one—sweating, exhausted people stumbling over a stretch of dusty road, attended by shouting crowds. He wondered if this new sport was some remote descendant of those. Perhaps it was the final perfected phase of it, as the new society was the perfected phase of the hideous confusion of the twentieth century. There must be wonderful athletes in such a world as this.

He had fallen into a reverie, looking into the green distance, when the sixth sense of being the object of scrutiny caused him to glance back at Ena. She had drawn a little farther away, and he caught her, so that she flushed, with her eyes running over him in a minute examination of limbs, shape, and head.

The flush brought tears to her eyes, and she remarked hurriedly, with a suspicion of petulance, "I don't think you would make a mountain racer: you are too thin." Then added a moment later with a bright, deliberate smile, "But I like fair hair!"

V

A voice dropped at them out of the sky.

"Hi there! Hi there!"

Guy started and glanced up. A tiny machine was hanging about a hundred feet above them. It must have come up noiselessly, for they had heard nothing—a small, flimsy-looking object with diminutive wings. It seemed extraordinary to Guy that it did not overbalance and pitch out the man who was craning recklessly out of it, projecting a flushed, dark face towards them. But the little silver contrivance remained perfectly still and level in what seemed a preposterous indifference to the laws of gravitation. Ena sprang to her feet.

The man saw that he had attracted their attention and called more quietly:

"Will you let me in? I'm sent from the Labourers' Bureau. One of your carriers registered wrong this morning."

"Oh yes, of course." Ena jerked and danced a little as she talked. "I'll go and switch it off." She threw an explanation at Guy. "We're insulated. On your account. For the last three days." She disappeared into the house.

Guy gazed up at the aeroplane, half understanding. The man had sat back in his seat, and a moment later it dropped gently like a settling bird on the grass beyond the terrace. Guy hurried towards it.

The man climbed out leisurely, lifting a leather case after him. He was a thick-set youth in working overalls, with a broad, blunt-nosed face. He surveyed Guy curiously in silence.

"You will not be the twentieth-century man they say they have here?" he demanded after a moment.

Guy admitted it. He was fascinated by the little machine, which was exquisite, like a silver insect. The man gasped and put his bag down on the grass.

"You're not jesting? Well… you look just like everyone else." He gazed at Guy disappointedly.

"What did you expect?" Guy smiled.

The man shook his head non-committally. "Well, it's wonderful what these doctors can do in these days, isn't it?" he remarked philosophically after a moment. "They were saying there was something queer going on here, but one never knows what's true. Only then they insulated the place. I can tell you there was many a one wanted to come on this job, but I had been without longest… I'll have something to tell them when I get back."

He seemed for the first time to realise Guy's interest in his machine, and his face brightened. "I suppose you'll not have seen one of these before? I can show you one for the first time!"

Guy laughed at the repetition of Ena's words; but before he had time to answer the other plunged into a stream of information with such zest of explanation that Guy found it difficult to follow him. The friendly, eager loquacity of these people confused him a little, even while it reassured. It seemed to give them a faintly foreign suggestion for him, in spite of their English voices. "Russian" was the word that occurred to him, although he had never known any Russians. Among the flood of technical details, anecdotes, sentiments, he made out that the thing was an "aerocycle," and provided the usual mode of getting about, but little else. He reflected that he would sometime have to find a teacher who would come down to his mental pace, but there was time enough for that. The days of hurry were over.

They heard Ena's voice calling and approaching through the house. The youth hesitated, with a funny, furtive glance in that direction. He put a hand on Guy's arm and began to draw him around the corner of the house.

"If you'll come with me to the cellar, where my job is, I'll tell you a lot more," he promised in an eager whisper.

Guy, laughing a little, for the manœuvre and the other's desire to keep his audience were of crystalline transparence, allowed himself to be drawn.

VI

The marvellous cellar revealed to Guy what had become of the cumbrous household apparatus for which he had looked in vain that morning. It had been banished underground like Solomon's earthbound genii, or like the human servants of the Victorian industrial era. But these were servants without the alloy of consciousness, unsupervised, discreet, silent, perfect.

In every direction tubes ran off, along which came and went the necessities of life from central kitchens, laundries, stores, and post-offices. The machinery was self-cleaning, self-lubricating, self-starting, self-stopping. The things ran themselves, as the workman said. At the rare times when, as now, some readjustment became necessary, the fact registered itself at a central depot where workmen were ready for the summons. But such summonses came less and less often as the devices were brought to perfection. The man told him that this had been his first job for days, though he always went to the depot in the mornings.

This much Guy gleaned out of a great deal that was unintelligible.

"I suppose," finally the workman stopped short in his task, which was some tightening of the parts in the appliance by means of which the loaded tray would rise into the dining-room above at mealtimes. He wrinkled his brow in mental effort, staring at Guy. "I suppose there wouldn't be any machinery in your time? Ha, ha, ha!" he laughed out suddenly. "You rode about on horses, didn't you?—I saw one last week—and could only speak as far as you could shout? And you wore long pants and bowler hats!... God! it must be wonderful for you!"

"We had automobiles and aeroplanes too, and sent wireless messages," said Guy sharply. In some curious manner it touched his vanity to be supposed to come from an age before machinery. "But we didn't have all that you have. And we had to be always watching to see that our machines didn't go wrong."

"Might almost as well be without them, I should say," the other grinned. "To think of hanging about a machine all day to see that it worked rightly! I remember they used to talk about the pre-automatic age at school. I suppose that's where you come from? Well, you'll find all that over long ago... I guess civilised life will seem pleasant to you after what you were used to."

The little adjustment was accomplished and the man sat down conversationally on a wooden slab.

"What is the thing that has surprised you most so far?" he demanded.

But before Guy had fairly set himself to the task of answering, he was telling him at length what were the things that he ought to find most surprising.

VII

It was Dr. Wayland himself who finally recovered Guy from the talkative mechanic, just when he was beginning to feel a trifle fatigued and bewildered. He noticed that the man fell silent as soon as the Doctor came into the room. It appeared that his own instinct of reverence for Dr. Wayland affected other people also, since there was here no question of employer and employed, of rich and poor. All that was over for ever. And yet the workman seemed actually to shrink a little as the Doctor's spare figure advanced across the room towards them, and he began to gather up his tools with the hurry of embarrassment. He said a comradely "Good-bye" to Guy, none the less, and wished the Doctor "Good day," to which the other responded courteously.

It was the end of Guy's first excursion into the outer world, for the Doctor would let him stay downstairs no longer for that day. They lunched together in the little room, and Guy told his friend, with the trustful, boyish frankness which seemed to be his birthright in the new world, of all that he had thought and felt.

"It is beautiful," he said. "And I think that half the beauty is in the ease of mind with which a chap can regard it. There is nothing to—harry one."

Dr. Wayland turned on him a look half enigmatic, half compassionate.

"There need never be anything to harry you again," he said quietly.

CHAPTER IV

A DIALOGUE OF THE CENTURIES

I

THE HANDING OVER OF HIS POWER-BOX WAS TO GUY A symbol which he could not pass without emotion. John Wayland gave it to him as they sat on the hillside overlooking the Wayland homestead and the river valley beyond; and to John Wayland, as Guy knew, it was a trivial and casual action. It was the very triviality and casualness of it, here and now, that made it for him so intensely significant. Yet he tried to receive it as John gave it—this little embodiment of wealth and power—as one man might accept a match from another; and he thought that he had succeeded. And then John's bright grey eyes turned upon him that swift glance of amusement that he was already learning to know.

John was like his uncle, Dr. Wayland, and this fact, no doubt, had bearings on his effect upon Guy. It was as if something of the Doctor's subtle influence, something of what Guy felt as the Doctor's participation in his personality, passed across to his nephew so far as the Doctor reappeared in him. So long as he lived in the Wayland household, Guy would know it instinctively if either of them came into a room where he was, though his own back might be turned.

But John Wayland's brilliant youth needed no borrowed effect.

If it had been John who had stepped out before him the day before, when he was waiting in wondering stillness for the human manifestation of the new world, instead of Ena's quaint little figure, he would have felt no incongruity. John Wayland's personality, even at the moment of introduction, affected him as with a spiritual recognition, a quick sensation of awed pain, almost like the beginning of love.

John was a dark young man, gay and instinct with life; the lines of his face were impetuous—an impetuosity reined in by the authority of a wide smooth forehead and a certain merry coolness in the grey eyes. He gave the effect of being finely tempered, like a slender sword meant for affairs of honour. In the carriage of his slim body was the most delicate suggestion of an arrogant swagger. The word that Guy wanted for him was not in his meagre French vocabulary, though he had always admired the quality with an almost morbid intensity. It was *insouciant*.

As soon as they had been introduced, John had carried him away in a sweep of gay comradeship up to this hillside perch, saying that he had a thousand questions to ask him, while Ena, trying to follow, in her schoolgirl habit of dogging always the members of the party most likely to prove entertaining, had been called back by her father. Up there the two young men lounged and smoked and talked the morning away.

II

Up there John had given him the power-box. Guy thanked him in a carefully nonchalant voice. And then John flashed that laughing glance at him.

"You are wondering whether you should not show 'proper pride' over this valuable gift?" he suggested. It was Guy's first experience of a penetration which was to delight and alarm him many times.

"No," he stammered hastily. "I know it's nothing. That is—" John laughed. He gave in. "Oh, you wouldn't understand. What it would have meant in the old times…"

"You must try me," John said. "That is what I want to know from you—I have always wanted to know it—what life was like then. One can't discover that from books. There, the most puzzling things of all are taken for granted, as if they were unalterable conditions of existence. I suppose it was always so; in the same way, it is difficult to enter the mind of a mediæval writer, to whom Heaven and Hell were fixed points on which hung everything else. Your fixed points were Poverty and Competition."

He began to question Guy about his own experience, questions which seemed to swoop like a hawk on skulking truths. It occurred to Guy, as he talked, that this was the first time a person of the new age had shown interest in anything he might have to tell. The others had seemed far more eager to impart information to him. He had been glad enough of this; and yet it gave him relief now to put into words those harrowing old days, which seemed to him by this time to be on the other side of a gulf, receding like a nightmare, while yet remaining vivid in his memory. But, though he told John of the twentieth-century London which he had known, he never approached the last days of his life there. Some inhibition always held him back from that. Nor did John ever press him on that point, or on any purely personal matter. It was the typical experience that his questions searched after, the everyday thoughts, actions, motives, attitude of the ordinary person under conditions that were to him so strange.

"It was the psychology of insecurity, all that," he said at last. "A vicious circle. You were poor, and so you could not stop to think. You did not think, therefore you were poor."

"What is it that you mean about 'thinking'?" Guy asked uncertainly.

"You must understand that we are actually a very unoriginal people in this twenty-second century. We have almost no things, moral or material, that were not already known in your day. But we are immensely better off, because we make use of them. In those days, as it seems to us, you tried your utmost to conceal and confine everything useful. You hid sources of power, processes, inventions from each other, like jealous lovers trying to sequester their mistresses. You were always working against each other, either individually or in cliques. Two or three factories making the same thing within a mile of each other would work with primitive machinery on insufficient capital; half-filled vehicles would go on the same journey almost side by side. It would be pathetic if it wasn't so funny. Imagine merely the amount of attention you compelled yourselves to waste on the most elementary matters—like a race of hypochondriacs who spent their time studying their own digestions."

Guy tingled under the banter. "We did not all admire the existing state of things, you know."

"Of course not," John returned quickly, with his disarming smile. "My manners are not actually so bad as to make an individual responsible for the follies of his century. God knows that I should not like to be held responsible for the follies of mine." He laughed a little.

"But to us," he continued, "you were like a person who prefers to go on putting up with a leaky basin rather than step over to the shelf to get another. But one sees how it really was. It was a question of fear. You dared not stop to think things out because of the stress of immediate poverty. You had to go on patching and botching and making shift because the outside pressure never gave you time to look up. Most of you never even saw the basin on the shelf."

"Do you mean that we might have had—all this," Guy spread his hands in a wide gesture to the countryside, "if we had chosen?"

"Certainly, most of it, if you had set about getting rich collectively instead of individually. Materials haven't altered much, only methods. We have much cheaper power, of course, than you had, because we can use free electricity. But that secret too would probably have been found long before your day if you had not starved your scientists. It is the cheapness of power that makes us able to spread our population comfortably. That would not have been much use, of course, if we had not learned to limit our population in the first place."

"That was already talked of in my time," said Guy.

"You talked of many things, I know," John laughed. "Yet one of the early Labour Governments actually tried paying for births, in spite of the warnings of an old economist druid—Baynes—or some such name. The East End of London, here, became like an over-ripe cheese, so the books say, so that they had to stop it in a panic. But, after that, people found out how to prevent births, and then women's egotism came to the rescue, just as men's egotism had created the problem in the first place. There was never any need for legislation. You won't find any large families now. And you won't find any crowded towns."

"That was one of the worst things," Guy burst out abruptly. "There was no room to move. People everywhere, always getting in the way, wherever you went, whatever you tried to do… It was worse, somehow, that they were like oneself."

John's interest seemed to draw from him, tumbling and incoherent, ideas that he had not known he possessed.

"Yes, I see that." He looked at Guy interestedly. "It must have encouraged the extra-consciousness obsession… You don't know our jargon. I mean by that the morbidly vivid realisation of the people round you each as a separate, complete consciousness, an endlessly repeated parody of oneself, like the Inquisition Torture of the Mirrors. If one ever realises that idea fully for the tenth part of a second, nothing can be more terrible."

"Yes. It was that. And then as well there was having to fight them and knowing that they were fighting you. Say that you got a job that you needed badly against other people who needed it too. You couldn't turn back; that would simply mean that you went under, as things were then. But you couldn't help realising it sometimes—I mean the other chap's existence, quite vividly, as you say. It was ghastly."

"Ah! You felt that too?" John's eyes dwelt on him a moment. "I should not have expected that. Not in those days… But you know that is part of the great 'sympathy' problem, Martin." He laughed. "I can't honestly claim that we have finally solved that, too. It has driven many a good brain distracted, and will drive many another yet… I suppose that to limit one's sympathies suitably will always be one condition of a happy life."

For a moment Guy felt a chill as if a cloud had come across the sun. But it passed as he looked out silently over the countryside. In this wider view it did not seem deserted, as he had felt it for a moment in the garden on the day before. Far away to the left, above the greenery, rose the towers of Westminster. On the reaches of the river that were within sight craft of various kinds passed from time to time; people walked on the white strips of road, and in other parallel roads occasional vehicles sped along. In the air, silent aeroplanes darted and danced like summer insects, and as beautiful and flashing. And yet it was a country scene, the gracious country of meadow and grove which is typically England. Buildings were more numerous than he had suspected, but each stood apart, innocent of smoke and dirt and litter, with no straggling out-buildings or tatter of hanging clothes. Red and grey and white, they contrasted harmoniously with the prevailing green. These human dwellings appeared—Guy felt the effect, though he could not have expressed it—what only rare happy accident had enabled them to appear in the old days, like natural objects, instead of excrescences, as much in place as a bird's nest in a bush. A vague suggestion of the implication that man, too, was now in key with Nature, in his right place as the final perfection of creation, no longer an alien, rested soothingly on Guy's mind, so that he turned to answer John's last words lightly.

"There can't be much need for sympathy now."

"You think not?" John smiled back.

"When everyone can have food and clothes and shelter without conditions, and all work is so light that every day is what we should have called a half-holiday! When you have no wars, and very little disease, and can prevent pain almost entirely! When no one suffers any disadvantages from his birth, and everyone has his chance!"

"Yes," said John thoughtfully, "everyone has his chance."

"And so all our old troubles are out of date."

"Yes. The centre of life has shifted. The things that you worried most about go on like one's breathing... I had already some
notion of your age's obsession with wealth-getting, having read old
literature. 'Money!' It seems to have been once almost as potent
a word as 'Love' or 'Art'!"

Again Guy felt for a moment the sharp touch of disdain; almost
the sting of injustice. It was impossible to make John Wayland
understand fully. How could a being grown up to such surroundings realise the truth of those terrible old times? It was a matter
of curiosity and amusement to him, like the queer, brutal rites
of some primitive tribe. He could see and laugh at the waste and
the folly; it was out of the question that he should ever reach
any consciousness of the actual process of living, of the terrors,
the miseries, the humiliations, worst of all, the ghastly sense
of one's own perversion as one was caught and ground in the
twentieth-century economic machine, which often, like ancient
torturers, left one's sight to the last, so that one might watch one's
own mutilation. And yet he longed to make John understand,
to compel him into identification with that old experience of
humanity, and, at the same time, contradictorily, desired to keep
him still untouched, free and careless. He realised inarticulately
what it essentially was—John had given him the clue himself—
that gave John his peculiar quality—that he had never known
fear. It made him beautiful and terrible. And for the moment,
as his emotion swung Guy back to that old time, so that his old
wounds ached like physical bruises, his sense of intenser experience made John also dimly pathetic to him, as if he were a child
beside a grown man.

The impression passed almost before it had developed. In these
clear, delightful days, serious or painful emotions were impossible

to Guy. They sheered off from his profound peacefulness of soul. He did not even miss anything of John's argument.

"It is like this," he was saying. "By your time everyone had some confidence in your system of justice. Of course, there would be jokes and grumbles, even obvious abuses; but, generally speaking, no one expected a judge or jury to be corrupt; nor could there be any serious dispute as to whether murder was a crime or not. All that had been fought out and settled long before in the Dark Ages, when murder might be a crime if one man committed it and not if another did, and when every ordinary right had to be maintained by fighting. Well, we have reached the same point in regard to economic matters as you had reached in regard to the administration of justice. A man no more worries now about where his livelihood is coming from than he worried in your time whether or no his next-door neighbour intended to murder him. It has dropped out of mind. The thing runs itself."

"The thing runs itself—"—that phrase seemed to recur. The mechanic in the cellar had used it also about the contrivances carrying on the work of the household; it seemed to be a fact that all that immense exercise of energy that had been devoted to the mere keeping alive—to feeding, clothing, housing, warming, conveying the human body—had been removed from the individual human being's sphere of responsibility—almost, as John said, dropped from his consciousness.

The thing ran itself—leaving men free. For what?

CHAPTER V

FARTHER AFIELD

I

"**Y**OU MUST LEAVE US SOMETHING TO PLAY WITH!"
John laughed at Guy's surprise at the number of
churches they were passing as they walked along the riverside
avenue above the sunken, swift-traffic road into town.

Like most of his "advanced" contemporaries in the early twentieth century, Guy had vaguely supposed that another hundred
years would see the end of Christianity, and all Europeans, at any
rate, intelligently agnostic. These towers and spires were out of
his picture of the new society, as if one should come upon a pine
tree in the Sahara.

"Your austerity for us was terrible," John reproached him. "I
know all about it from your books. No tobacco, no alcohol, veg-
etarian diet, no religion…! Did you really think yourselves capable
of propagating a race like that? Aren't you relieved, after all, to
find us still so human?"

"I'm glad about the tobacco," Guy confessed.

"Then you mustn't begrudge other people their religion," said
John. "Monasticism, Christian and Buddhist, is one of our most
popular hobbies."

"Buddhist!"

"Yes, plenty of that. Buddhism was only beginning to

make headway here in your time, wasn't it? It was what saved Christianity—at least, that is the general opinion. It drove most of the little sects back to Rome. There's nothing like a common enemy to reconcile differences! The great movement into religious orders is more recent—since the easier times began. Naturally, all this doesn't affect intellectuals much—only in our slang and our expletives, as you must have noticed."

"But who—?" Guy broke off abruptly. His sense of propriety vanished in astonishment; he stood still and stared.

Although he had never travelled, he recognised at once the object that was approaching. It was a woman of the East in a litter carried by bearers. Through the gorgeous, partly drawn curtains he could see the white draperies and the gleaming eyes peeping over a veil which concealed the lower part of the face. And, precisely as if he were living in a twentieth-century magazine story, just as it swung past, the figure bent forward and flashed at him, as he stood in the road, a bright, shy glance.

John, shaking with laughter, pulled him away quickly.

"Oh, Guy, you must—you must—learn not to be so naïve. It is nothing but a harem woman."

"A harem woman? From Turkey?"

"God, no! From England. They don't exist in Turkey now."

"Then what on earth—?"

"It is only a fashion… And if you mean to ask me to explain fashions to you as well as everything else, I shall resign my position."

"But everyone doesn't—?"

"No, no. It has almost passed out now. But it was very much in vogue among normal women a few years ago. They used to shut themselves up in a special part of the house and never allow any men except their husbands and sons to come near them. When they went out, it was in litters like this one. Some men liked it too. A few used to spend all their coupons in maintaining several women shut up like that, and some even let their daughters marry men they had never seen. However, it soon worked itself out. They bored themselves with it, and wanted to see more of the world again. And the jealousy between the wives was making the men neurasthenic wrecks; you see, the women wouldn't, actually, most of them, submit to the beatings necessary for the success of that régime... At one time," he added casually, "Agatha Wayland wanted to bring Ena up as a harem woman, but my uncle wouldn't consent."

"I should think not, indeed," exclaimed Guy indignantly. This new aspect of Agatha Wayland, his host's wife, whom, with her broad matronly face and figure, her alternating fits of chatter and apathy, he had hitherto regarded as an amiable nonentity, disconcerted him. "Surely your society doesn't encourage a fashion of that kind?" he added. "If you come to that, where did they get those bearers?"

John laughed softly to himself. "You are making twentieth-century psychology much clearer to me, Martin. You are so anxious that everyone should be free, yet you wouldn't leave them free to be harem women, if they chose... As to the bearers, the State is bound to provide any goods or labour that is demanded by a certain minimum of coupon-holders, so long as no necessary service suffers by it. That was settled by the Consumers' Minority Act, which is a date one has to learn at school, like Magna Charta or Habeas Corpus."

"I see." Guy fell silent, reflecting.

"I believe that you will find our fashions more extravagant than yours used to be," said John; "except among your very richest, perhaps. Some of your American millionaires seem to have had quite modern ideas... You see, we are all rich now... However, there remains this to say: our fashions are genuine fashions; they occur because they please people, not because someone wants to sell something, or because someone wants to show that he is richer than his neighbours."

For a moment an appreciation of ramifications and consequences beyond anything he had yet imagined overwhelmed Guy. It was the same sensation as he had felt in his schooldays when a sum, probably wrong from the beginning, was developing enormous sequences of figures beyond the stretch of the childish brain.

John glanced at him, and seized his arm with a friendly, reassuring laugh. "It hadn't occurred to you," he suggested, "that social freedom meant also freedom to be the sort of fool one wanted?"

II

They came to the Bachelor Chambers where John lived during his vacations. Close by, Guy recognised, with a start, Blackfriars Bridge, still spanning the river. It looked immeasurably strange, standing there unaltered in this park-like country with its long tree-shaded avenues and stretches of turf. It was almost a relief to turn away from it and all its implications, as they passed up a broad gravel drive to where the Chambers stood back from the river. It was an attractive building, aiming at and achieving solidity, as the Wayland house aimed at and achieved delicacy and lightness. Grey stone and red creepers gave it an appearance of age; but John told him that it had been built less than a hundred years. As they approached from the riverside, it looked like an old priory or college.

There were young men everywhere, lounging in the garden, swimming or rowing on the river in front, rising noiselessly on aerocycles. One tiny machine even leapt from a high window as they watched, and, springing skywards, vanished with astonishing speed. A bunch of heads with open, laughing mouths and a waving confusion of arms protruded after it from the window.

"Not an easy trick, that," John explained. "I expect it was a bet."

At lunch in the large, cool dining-room, two of John's friends came to complete their table—one a solemn-looking, heavy, blonde young man, who, however, became cheerful after his second glass of beer; the other more like John himself, with a keen dark face and a lively manner. They greeted Guy with the tact of a complete casualness, and began to talk as if there were no stranger present. He would, indeed, have supposed that they had no idea how much a stranger he was, that John had not prepared them with any account of him, but that, every now and then, when their crowding allusions bewildered him, one or other would break off to make him an explanation—to characterise a person, or describe some social adjustment. They both seemed to have in some degree John's talent for clear exposition—the power of presenting important facts without encumbering detail, of divining, too, the mental position of their hearer.

But all explanations ceased when John and Alexis, the dark youth, became involved in an incomprehensible argument about someone whom they called a Vibrationist and his Art Calculus. Even when John explained the subject to him at another time, Guy's mind jibbed at it and lapsed into confusion. He gathered only that art—pictorial effects—æsthetic impressions of all kinds, were now threatening—or promising, as it seemed to John's taste—to resolve themselves into a matter of mathematics, to become calculable, as had sound effects long before; he even understood dimly that John believed that all reality might ultimately become amenable to mathematical analysis. But at present he was entirely at sea. The combatants attacked each other like gamecocks, without pause or mercy. Short, quick sentences flashed and stabbed. He noticed that heads were turning at the neighbouring tables, grins and nudges passing round. Obviously, the duel was not the first of its kind. But John and Alexis, whole-hearted as hounds on the scent, might have been alone together in space.

Hartland, the fourth member of the party, smiled across at Guy in an appeal for sympathetic enjoyment. The smile made his large, rather solemn face, with its wide blue eyes, instantly charming and innocent. Getting Guy's laughing response, he unexpectedly raised his glass to him with a slight bow suggestive of a foreign politeness.

The little action curiously conveyed to Guy a completer sense of welcome and ease than he had felt before. The fact that he instinctively returned the greeting also gave him a strange pleasure. In some way the movement in itself seemed to make him free of a world of youth and courtesy and charm, of combined bold freedom and graceful play. It was the realisation of his old inarticulate dreams of graceful living, which had never come into practical touch with his own crude, hard-pressed, incoherent personality.

The word-battle stopped at last as abruptly as it had begun. Lunch was over and the room was almost empty. John glanced round and broke off with some jest about his dignity before his pupil. Alexis got up reluctantly, and anxiously invited him to come and finish the argument the next afternoon.

His dark eyes were shining; one might suppose that he believed the fate of worlds to depend upon the issue.

"You speak as if arguments were ever finished," John laughed at him. "You Russians are all alike. You will never rid yourselves of your belief in ultimate truth. But I will come."

Hartland put an arm through John's and drew him ahead as they walked down to the river again. Alexis, following with Guy, poured into his bewildered ears a flood of metaphysical argument.

They had decided to return by water. John rejected with scorn the row of power canoes and chose a light wooden shell innocent of machinery. With much splashing and laughter, they got Guy, who had never been in a canoe before, against a pile of cushions in the bow. They pushed off, John and Alexis shouting repartees at each other as the distance increased.

III

Guy lounged in the canoe, steeped in sunshine, a little languid after his first walk, and watched the fascinating miniature whirlpools go spinning backwards from John's vigorous paddle. He felt a wonderful sense of well-being. The beauty of carelessness had hold upon him for the first time in his life. The canoe, light, fragile, detached, seemed an exquisite little world in itself. He watched John's brooding face with affection, wondering what he was thinking of. There was a longer period of silence between them than ever before in their curious companionship.

John answered the unspoken question at last, throwing off his preoccupation with a shaking of his sleek, black head.

"Are you troubled with after-wit, Martin?" he inquired. "I know precisely now what I ought to have said to Alexis a quarter of an hour ago… It will never be said now. He will never give me the same opening again." He mourned a moment over his lost opportunities, and then asked Guy if he had liked the Chambers. "You will, perhaps, like to live there sometime later," he suggested. "At present I know that you will not wish to leave my uncle."

Guy realised to his surprise that this was true. Enchanted as he was by the place, it seemed impossible that he should live out of the immediate neighbourhood of Dr. Wayland. But he did not exert himself to discover the reason for this certainty, nor how John had guessed it. The moment was too pleasant for questionings.

"Come and go as it pleases you," John told him. "You know by this time that your mere existence gives you a right to be there— there is always room enough… Hartland hopes to see you again when he can talk to you alone. You puzzled him a little."

"That's natural, isn't it?" Guy shrugged his shoulders, smiling.

"Ah yes! of course, you interest everyone. But I meant in a more special manner. He is a philologist—half-German, naturally—and your speech puzzled him. He said that it was generally accepted that pronunciation had altered somewhat since the twentieth century, though your phonetic systems are so confusing, being, like everything else in your time, in a state of civil war, that it is difficult to be certain. But you speak just as we do."

Guy sat up suddenly at the last sentence, causing the canoe to rock perilously. "Why, of course," he laughed excitedly, "I never noticed it before. You all talk with a Cockney accent!" And the laugh continued, independent of his will, on a high note.

A violent bump of the nose of the boat just behind him, a few seconds later, jolted him into soberness.

"Pardon," said John placidly; "it is not often that I am so clumsy. Will you take the other paddle and push us off?" They had run into a jutting piece of the bank.

Guy drew the paddle to him gingerly and began to press back against the turf. But a canoe, like a bicycle, requires a trained sense of balance. He pushed too hard, and the side of the boat nearest to the bank dipped suddenly. Instinctively, he threw himself over in the opposite direction, and the canoe tilted over with him, dipping its side almost to the surface of the water, so that he was within an ace of pitching out. Then it righted itself.

"Thank you," John's voice from the stern contained a hint of amusement. He was still erectly balanced on his high seat. "I think you had best keep still now." He gave a few vigorous reverse strokes and, the next moment, they were again speeding down with the current.

"Now," said John, with a smile that frankly gave his stratagem away, "you feel better, so we will thrash out this small matter... It seems necessary. I think you meant to say that your own speech was not the standard speech of your time."

At the moment Guy did not recognise the leap which his companion's mind must have taken, though it gave him matter for wonder afterwards.

"That is true," he was able to answer almost calmly. The physical activity had acted like a spray of cold water on his agitation. "I belonged to the lower classes—that is, the lower middle class—and I could never get my speech to be quite like that of—of—the 'best' people—though I tried." He gave John a sickly smile, but felt impelled to go on. "I think, all the same, I never fully admitted to myself that there was any difference."

"A nasty mess, that," John said, after a pause, looking at him thoughtfully. "Deep enough to escape even my uncle. I am glad we had it out."

It occurred to Guy that he was speaking as if of a decaying tooth.

"People should help each other to get rid of these mental parasites... Oh yes! We still have such, though not, of course, this kind... There are very few people alive now who would have understood your trouble at all. To come back to the point, you were, in fact, ahead of your time. I see plainly now how it must have been. London speech has exercised a constant slow drag on standard English speech—it always did that, I believe—so that we are now at the point which you reached in struggling towards the standard of your time. Hartland will interest himself in this intensely."

Guy had followed him but vaguely, and was glad when he became silent again. The stir and trouble of his confession, subsiding, was succeeded by the ease of mental purgation. The moment was too good for thought or for discussion. Something that had oppressed him all his life had gone for ever; he felt free and light as air. His delicious mood returned, perfected, and in a bliss of mental and bodily ease he watched the trees and houses sliding past, listened to the sweep of John's paddle and the tinkle of falling drops, and to the more distant splash of a rowing-boat going up-stream.

It seemed to him that one such day was enough to heal and reconcile all miseries; the mere fact that such loveliness should be possible at some time, in some place, seemed sufficient compensation for all the ugliness and confusion and pain of all the centuries. At last, in this wonderful new world into which incredible good fortune had dropped him, life had become all charm. And, even as he thought it, he knew also that the peculiar beauty of this one moment could never return. But the moment was so perfect that, until they actually touched the landing-stage opposite Dr. Wayland's house, no regret rose in his heart.

CHAPTER VI

DISTINCTIONS

I

IT DISCONCERTED GUY SLIGHTLY TO DISCOVER THAT JOHN WAS engaged to be married. Yet not precisely engaged, it seemed. John himself had put it, in introducing the subject of Sylvia Grant, who wanted to meet Guy:

"We are in love with each other at present. We may even marry."

Guy knew that he ought not to be startled at the casual-sounding statement. It was in accordance with what he should expect in an enlightened society—the attitude on sex matters that had always been set up as an ideal (though rarely attained) at his Socialist Club. On the other hand, no one had supposed that marriage as an institution, any more than religion, would survive the next fifty years. He had already found that there existed, at any rate, some examples of it in the new age, but it did not seem to hold the same position as of old. And Guy had been accustomed to people who, however enlightened, were either engaged to be married, or else were not.

There was another element in his slight discomfiture. This new disclosure seemed to compromise the peculiar quality of detachment in John which had caught his imagination. Guy could not think of him as held by any tie, even the most fragile; he was reluctant to admit the idea. Sylvia Grant's existence came as an intrusion on their careless life of ranging talk and exploration.

He answered a little stiffly that he would be pleased to meet Miss Grant, causing John to smile at the prefix.

"She is a delightful actress and a charming person," John assured him. "Intellectual, of course."

It struck Guy as a curious description to be applied to an actress.

"You use that word more than we did," he said.

"Do we? Yes, no doubt we do. It must be so, of course. You see, the distinction between intellectual and unintellectual necessarily appears much more strongly now than it did in your time. That is the natural result of the difference in our mode of life. No one now is prevented from following his own bent, or forced to follow some other. Everyone can have as much education as he can tolerate, so that the real quality of a person is able to appear. In your days, it must often have been difficult to discover the quality of a person at all. In fact, I imagine you made very little attempt at mental measurement of any kind?"

"There were examinations," Guy said doubtfully. "I remember I sometimes read about psychological tests too."

"Read?" John laughed. "Well, in these days, we have many ways of measuring degrees of consciousness. Those are infinite in number, of course; but, in general, our way of life tends to draw a line between those above a certain level and those beneath it—and to widen the gap. In other words, intellectuals tend to become more intellectual and unintellectuals ('normals' we call them, for distinction), less so. You see, it must fall out that way, since everyone who is sufficiently interested in things of the intellect to pursue them for their own sake is able to do so, while those who are not sufficiently interested are driven by no necessity."

"Then, do you find that everybody falls into one class or the other?"

"Most people. It is a rough-and-ready division, but convenient. There are many border-line cases, pseudo-intellectuals—publicists mainly, and some who cut right across the division. Musicians are apt to make themselves awkward in that way. On the other hand, intermarriages between intellectuals and normals become rarer, and that helps to keep the classes distinct. It is found that the children in such marriages frequently revert to normality, and that naturally makes us intellectuals cautious. My uncle's family is an instance of a mixed marriage."

Several little outstanding perplexities which Guy had accumulated in the course of the new life began to fall into their places—Ena's statement that she was not going to be an "intellectual"; her suggestion to himself that her father would have preferred John to Terry as a son; some of the young men's talk at the Chambers.

"You may guess," John continued with his candid smile, "that I have been trying to class you, ever since I first saw you; but I confess that I have not succeeded. Another evidence that the distinction was less definite in your day."

Guy shivered with goose flesh. Any approach to the subject of his own personality affected him always now as with a slight physical chill and a mental recoil.

II

Guy's faint stir of antagonism did not long survive Sylvia Grant's presence. Her small quiet face with its candid eyes and firm little mouth placed her so delicately apart that it was impossible to think of her as an appendage to anyone. The clumsinesses which had always, in Guy's experience, been associated with any form of love-making, and in which he had unconsciously been dreading to see John involved, vanished with the other old nightmares into the limbo of the past. Only the same frank friendliness as John's manner had always shown to Guy himself, John and Sylvia expressed in their manner towards each other.

Sylvia's "intellectualism" seemed to be of a less positive and more tranquil character than John's, and yet, without any obvious reason, her coming brought into the house the little wave and stir that alters the quality of the psychological atmosphere and is felt like a change of weather out of doors—when a breeze begins to blow up on an oppressive afternoon, or when the sun suddenly pierces a clinging mist.

Her woman's tact, unlike the masculine tact of the young men at the Chambers, went straight to the point of Guy's peculiar position, acknowledged and placed the peculiarity by mentioning it at once and making of it an occasion for interest and admiration. One of her remarks remained in his mind:

"You have a chance to attain wisdom that no one has ever had before—a marvellous means of comparison. You will know what is essential and what vanishes. You have two planes of experience. Isn't that why people who have lived in two countries show an intellectual stamp one never finds in those who have lived in only one? But to live in two centuries! That must be like having a glimpse into the fourth dimension."

Guy hesitated, a little awed. Her attitude seemed strange after the pleasant, kindly tolerance to which he had become accustomed in the new age. He made a little gesture of appeal and helplessness.

"It's the other way," he said. "You all seem so much wiser than I am."

"Only in our own generation," John asserted, laughing.

It was the dinner hour while they were still talking, and Sylvia went in with them, John signalling the presence of two more persons to the Central Restaurant. Guy was becoming accustomed to the absence of the formality and of the polite compulsions which had been so prevalent in his own time, and especially in his own class. One of John's most illuminating expositions had worked out the connection between codes of manners and family kitchens.

But in spite of his familiarity with the easy coming and going of the new age, it seemed strange to him that Agatha and Ena Wayland should never before have met Sylvia Grant, John's probable future wife, as now appeared in John's brief introduction. Yet, why not? since it was himself and his experiences that had interested Sylvia. Those burdensome old family sentiments, based on the necessity for economic defence, had, of course, gone with the other burdens.

John was inquiring for his uncle, who had not appeared.

"He never comes to meals with us now," complained Agatha Wayland. "He always gets them in the laboratory. He…"

"I'll see if I can get him." John was out of the room before her sentence was completed.

"He'll come for John when he won't come for anyone else." Agatha turned to Sylvia for sympathy. "We've hardly seen him during the last weeks, except for a few days when Martin first came. His own family don't seem to be of any interest to him…"

"But he is engaged on some very important experiments, isn't he?" Sylvia interrupted. It was always necessary to interrupt Agatha, if one were to answer her at all.

"He's always engaged on something," said Agatha vaguely. "I often say I might as well not be married at all…"

"Why don't you get a divorce, then, mother?" Ena giggled.

John came back with Dr. Wayland; and the conversational balance shifted, as Guy had discovered that it always did when the Doctor came into the room, whether he took any part in the talk or not. John and Sylvia, with Guy's help, began to draw contrasts between the theatre of the present time and that of two centuries past. In one pause, Agatha asked John and Sylvia whether they meant to go to the Mountain Race on the next day, but Sylvia said that she had a rehearsal and John said that he never went. After that, Agatha lapsed again into her gentle taciturnity.

Ena, on the other hand, although she contributed nothing, followed the conversation with bright eyes, or, rather, Guy remembered afterwards an impression that she was watching the speakers rather than following what they said.

"And you actually saw plays acted with living people in the parts?" Sylvia demanded of Guy.

Guy assured her that he had. He had already seen one of the modern stereomovie plays, a development of the cinematograph in which colour, solidity, and sound had been added, giving so complete an illusion of reality that it had long ago superseded drama requiring the personal presence of the actors.

"And they acted the same parts night after night for months together? It's incredible. Like burning down a house every time one wanted to roast pork."

A shrill laugh from Ena, who evidently did not recognise the allusion, but thought it to be original, struck Guy's ear intrusively.

"And they didn't go crazy?" Sylvia demanded.

"I believe they did sometimes. There was gossip of that sort. But, on the whole, I think they liked it. They were in personal touch with their audiences, you see. I remember they thought a great deal of that."

"So do I," said Sylvia. "So do I. There is nothing more enlightening than to sit in the audience and watch one's own effects." She gave a little rueful grimace. "But your actresses can never even have heard themselves speak from outside: or had you phonographs then?"

"We had," said Guy; "but no one would have liked to think that his voice was similar to one."

"I heard an old twentieth-century phonograph at the museum a few days ago," said John. "It was like a crow with an attack of croup."

"And yet they went on!" said Sylvia. "Wonderful people! It is almost worse to think of than operations without anæsthetics. The audacity of it! To act, day after day, never knowing how you looked or sounded, except for the little truth you could sieve out of the lies people told you."

Guy told her all he knew about the theatres of his day, while Dr. Wayland and John listened interestedly. It was meagre, but, in conversation with Sylvia, it seemed more than it was. Words came fluently to him; she asked the right questions. He felt in himself a descriptive talent which he had never suspected before.

After dinner was over they had moved into a little lounge-room, a light rain preventing an evening on the veranda. Sylvia drew Guy into the window to a seat beside her, still talking eagerly. She had just discovered that he had seen Ellen Terry in her old age play the nurse in *Romeo and Juliet*. John and Dr. Wayland followed them, while Agatha sat in a cushioned armchair at a little distance with her hands in her lap. Later Guy realised what it was that he missed about her—she should have had a lapful of stockings and a needle of darning wool.

"Charm," said Sylvia, "is the one thing that John and his kind cannot analyse."

She exchanged with John one of the swift, humorous glances which seemed to be their habitual mode of communication. Seeing it, Guy felt less sure of his decision that there was nothing but friendship between them. It gave him a little shock of beauty, this quick flashing of a smile between the two pairs of young eyes. For the space of a second it seemed a thing all-sufficient in itself, like the exquisite moments in the canoe coming down the river. Then Sylvia turned back to Guy.

Ena was handing coffee cups. With a jerky movement she spilt a little on Sylvia's tunic of peach-coloured silk, apologised vehemently, and went down on her knees to mop at it with her handkerchief.

"Please don't mind," Sylvia smiled at her. "I shall have time to choose another to-morrow morning. Now, if I had lived in Martin's time, doubtless it would have been a serious matter. I suppose John would have had to 'stump up'"—she gave a delicious flavour to the obsolete slang phrase—"wouldn't he, Martin?"

But Ena's loud exclamations of horror and contrition continued, as they examined the damage. They jarred on Guy's ears, reminding him vaguely, in their exaggerated inflections, of the upper-middle-class girls of the twentieth century whom he had occasionally heard in the restaurants when he was being unusually extravagant, or they were being unusually economical. Their dramatic-toned "How perfectly topping's!" and "Isn't it too sweet's?" had always aroused in him a quite disproportionate surge of class antagonism. Ena was talking in that way now.

Then the little incident was over. Ena got up abruptly and, going to a low stool that stood back against the wall, sat down with a sudden air of reflective aloofness.

Dr. Wayland addressed Sylvia pleasantly:

"I hear you are going to marry this fortunate nephew of mine." The glance he threw towards John was touched incongruously, as it seemed to Guy, with some emotion almost painful.

Sylvia said frankly, "We haven't quite decided yet about marrying."

"We might change our minds about each other," said John, with another quick interchange of glances with her.

The Doctor smiled. "Well, if you will take my advice, you will marry," he said. The usual kindly confidence in his voice made Guy think that his earlier impression must have been mistaken. "I am convinced that it is better both for artists and for men of science. Some obligation to stability in one's emotions leaves one's mind so much freer. Casual unions are well enough for normals… And if either of you should develop a *grande passion*—well! you are both intelligent people. You can handle that when it happens. But I daresay you won't."

The little group beside the window had again become pleasantly absorbed in itself and its conversation. It turned, disconcerted, half vexed, as Ena Wayland, rising from her stool, advanced suddenly into the midst of it, planting herself in front of her father. Something deliberate in her gait and manner forced their attention, causing the conversation to break off abruptly. On her face was a sort of conscious ecstasy.

"Father," she said slowly, "I have decided to become a nun."

Dr. Wayland frowned. "We can talk about that later, Ena," he said.

Agatha Wayland had started and turned round in her chair, staring dumbly. John and Sylvia, after the first second, turned immediately away towards the window and began talking quietly together.

Ena looked round at her audience as if with a benignant scorn. "You don't understand," she exclaimed. "How could you?" She began to speak more and more quickly, her voice rising. "It is my whole life that I am giving up. I am going to bury my youth behind the grey walls of a convent. It will be all fasts and vigils and penances. I shall pray for all of you, and perhaps you will be saved by my prayers, though you will never know it... I have hesitated for a long time. I only felt certain of my vocation just now, while I was listening to your worldly talk. And now at last I know—I know..."

Her eyes turned upwards ecstatically.

Agatha Wayland broke into sobbing. "My little girl!... Ena!... My little girl!"

Dr. Wayland spoke with a cutting precision. "Whatever you know, you should know better than to interrupt my conversation with my guests."

There was a second's silence, while the chilling words seemed to re-echo in the room. Then Ena's expression of rapt certainty crumbled. Her lips wavered, her small face crumpled into wrinkles; suddenly she began to cry out hysterically:

"What do you care? What do any of you care? I'm going away. I shall be shut up all my life. I shall never see a man again. I helped Guy Martin when he came here... He didn't know anything... I showed him his first power-box. He wouldn't have known anything if it hadn't been for me. And all he cares about—all he cares about…" The words became strangled and incoherent. She dropped to the floor in a sobbing, weltering heap.

Dr. Wayland got up with an expression of resigned exasperation, raised her not ungently and, passing an arm under her shoulders, took her from the room. Agatha Wayland tried to follow, but he turned her back with a curt word.

The room seemed suddenly peaceful and empty. The two in the window-seat turned round again without a sign of disturbance.

"I began to be afraid when I saw the incident of the coffee," John smiled.

Sylvia murmured, "Poor child!"

Agatha Wayland glanced at them distractedly, then sat down again, wringing her hands together.

Sylvia began a flow of superficial chatter, and Guy recognised gratefully that she was helping to cover his own complete disconcertment. It was no more than necessary. Ena's outburst, and especially the fierce words that she had flung at himself, the sudden upheaval of the smooth social surface which the new age had shown him, gave him the sick alarm of a first earthquake shock. All had become a chaos of uncertainty; forces of which he knew nothing seemed to be at work, and might burst into action on any side at any moment. It was pleasant to hear the sympathy in John's and Sylvia's quiet voices. They, at any rate, seemed stable.

After a little time they rose to go. Dr. Wayland came down again as they were leaving; Guy heard him murmur an apology and Sylvia's clear reply:

"Of course I understand, Dr. Wayland. Your young daughter is beginning to grow up, and we thoughtlessly put a strain on her… Good-bye. I think we shall take your advice." She glanced confidingly up at him. Then she gave Guy, without speaking, a smile of delightful friendliness, and followed John out into the night.

III

Dr. Wayland came back into the room with a set expression. He glanced at his wife, still sitting idle in her chair, then doubtfully at Guy, and compressed his lips. Then the impulse to speak visibly conquered.

He spoke, however, in tones of considered moderation.

"Agatha, you should have told me you were letting her go to the priest. I found a scourge in her room."

Agatha gave a little cry, and clasped her hands convulsively.

"My little girl! To dedicate herself to God!"

"If she will accept my suggestion," said Dr. Wayland, still with the same deliberate restraint, "she will go instead, immediately her next birthday comes, to the Domestic Labour Bureau and begin her course as a worker."

Agatha began to sob again between her words. "Robert, you know how delicate she is. She couldn't work… And they have too many. I know… They can't keep them all occupied now."

Dr. Wayland laughed sardonically. "Then the work can't be so very arduous. In any case, it will scarcely be so hard as the life of a Poor Clare, which I understand to be Father Bradwen's suggestion. But I have removed that maggot for the present, anyhow."

He turned back to where Guy was standing, adrift and staring, and laughed more pleasantly.

"Come, Martin. These scenes are not good for you yet. But you will see that we also have our little difficulties sometimes—very small ones—nothing approaching what yours used to be—just enough to give a flavour to life. I am going to take you up to bed. If you mean to go to the Mountain Race to-morrow, you will need your sleep."

As they went up the stairs, Guy stammered out a few words.

"Miss—Ena—seems to have taken a dislike to me, I am afraid—perhaps…"

The Doctor glanced at him curiously, then laughed again. "Nonsense!" he said. "You know better than to take a girl's hysterics seriously. Women are liable to these little brain-storms, you know, especially when they are about Ena's age. You have never had a sister, have you? That accounts for it. Just behave as if nothing had happened, Martin, and you will find that nothing has."

The Doctor's voice rather than his words seemed to place the incident away in its right perspective. In a few moments Guy was ready to laugh at himself. An imaginative young girl, a little overwrought, had talked extravagantly. It was not a matter to think twice about. Before the Doctor left him, Guy was ready to fall into a quiet sleep as soon as his head touched the pillow.

CHAPTER VII

MOUNTAIN RACING

I

G UY AWOKE TO A MORNING OF SUNSHINE AND FRESHNESS
after the rain. He had learned by this time that it had become
possible to control the milder phases of the weather to some
extent—in particular, that unwanted rain could often be brought
down over the ocean by a release of power high in the air, so that
the summer of England, and of Western Europe generally, now
approached what only idealists in the twentieth century had supposed it to be.

It was, therefore, not surprising that the day of the great
International Mountain Race should be fine; but Guy wondered
whether the little breeze that blew in at the open side of his
room and cooled his forehead as he sat up in bed could have been
concocted by any meteorological skill. It seemed too sweetly
spontaneous.

He pressed a button by his bedside and lay back for a few
moments in unthinking enjoyment, until, after a warning buzz,
a wooden shutter dropped out from the wall in front of him and
a tray of coffee and rolls slid out upon it.

As he breakfasted in the Continental fashion which England
had now adopted, he thought of John and Sylvia, and of their love
affair, and found it pleasant. It came to him freshly, as if it were

the first love affair which had ever come within his experience. If he had known of them, other than in stumbling, line by line, schoolboy construing, he might have thought of the charming legendary loves of the ancient world, of Eros and Psyche, of the tales of nymphs and gods, for it was an impression of this kind that he had received: an impression of freshness and beauty, of an exquisite relationship, perfect in itself, unpolluted by any sordid association.

He realised presently that this, none the less, was the modern equivalent for the twentieth-century love affairs that he had known, and was amazed that it should seem to have so little in common with them. He looked back at those muddy confusions as an educated Hindoo might look at the hundred-armed Kali. Love affairs then had been matters of grinnings and gossip—whether so-and-so would succeed in catching so-and-so; jocular warnings against incurring breach of promise actions; "stumping up" for theatres and chocolates. Then, when the engagement was actually accomplished, came the shamefaced requests for rises in salaries; jiltings of the fellow who earned less for the fellow who earned more; quarrels and "will-shakings" by embittered parents; high-flown declarations leading to misery, "I wouldn't let *my* wife go out to work"; estimates passing round in winks and whispers as to the value of the ring. If there had been any element of sweetness in the business in its beginning, it would be effectually vulgarised before it had gone far. And yet Guy, like many of his kind, had always kept alive, underneath the snickerings and the nudges, an ideal conception of love—a conception which, more foolish than the rest, he had once tried to turn into a reality. But he hardly thought of that now; it was like an old nightmare remembered indistinctly and without emotion.

The money element gone, the vulgarity had gone too, quite magically. Disinterested love presented no surface for gibes or innuendoes. It was like a warmer, a special kind of friendship. And then he remembered how often, in the old days, friendships had been affairs of "tips" and "lifts," and came back again in thought to the Bachelor Chambers and John's life there.

As he dressed and put on the new tweeds which she had helped him to choose the day before, he thought also of Ena and smiled indulgently. It had been absurd of him to be taken aback by her behaviour on the previous evening. No doubt, as the Doctor had hinted, it was "all nerves." The convenient phrase sprang up to him out of his former life. His mother had early impressed upon him the conviction that women had nerves in another sense than men, and to this he had always attributed everything that he did not understand in women, not without some pleasurable sense of masculine superiority. He must be as kind to her as possible, to show that he had not taken offence.

The silent clock told him that he must meet Agatha and Ena for the start in half an hour. He hurried with his dressing, his new tweed costume rousing in him the tingle of adventure. It would be his first flight and the first time that he had been out of England.

II

In the big square from which the Leviathan planes were starting were more people than Guy had ever seen together since he had awakened in the new age. The great machines filled immediately as they stood in line, and rose directly up from the ground like birds, without requiring the preliminary run of the twentieth-century aeroplane. One could see them streaming away to the east as far as the eye could reach.

Agatha, bustling agitatedly, tried to get them into a plane that had filled as they approached it, meanwhile missing the next one also, and at last let Guy, laughingly, steer her to one farther down the line which was still empty. In the meantime he tried vainly to persuade her that both his statements—that there had been aeroplanes in his time, and that he had never been in one—were true. But she hastened away from the topic, generously trying to cover what she obviously thought to be mental confusion on his part. He had to give up the point at last, half pleased that the inequalities of competitive society should now be so utterly inconceivable to the ordinary person, half irritated by her want of comprehension.

As they climbed in, with Ena following, he was disappointed to find that passengers all travelled in a covered saloon, though he realised later that the pace would be too great for anyone to endure the rush of air outside. He obtained a seat by the window with Agatha chattering excitedly beside him. Ena, who was pale and subdued this morning and had persistently refused to meet his eyes, took a place at the far side of the saloon, in spite of her mother's emphatic signals, and was at once separated from them by a rush of passengers.

Guy felt sorry for her, but quickly forgot all about her in the interest of the new experience. The window beside him had an outward slope, and he was able to see something of the country beneath as it scurried from under them at an astonishing pace. The great machine flew without swaying and with only the faintest vibration.

His fellow-passengers were obviously in an excited frame of mind. There was much talk and laughter, and voices rose almost hysterically. He realised afresh as he glanced round, what he already knew theoretically, how completely social distinctions had disappeared. Everyone was well dressed. There was variation in style and colour and taste, but little in cleanliness or quality. All the voices in the medley spoke with the same accent and idiom. The only difference remaining was in the things said; but there, as John had pointed out, the quality of the speaker came out with all the more startling distinctness.

Gradually, through the general buzz, there distinguished itself the tones of a slightly affected tenor voice just behind him.

"Terry's a good horse, but, after all, he's still a younker. I fancy the Von for one year more."

"Ready to back your opinion?" The other voice, also that of a young man, suggested a suppressed eagerness.

"Anything in reason," the first speaker laughed quietly.

"Will you stake Molly against Beatrix Smedley?"

"Oh, well—I don't know—that's heavy odds... Ha, ha, ha! You've set your heart on getting her, haven't you?"

There was a second's pause, and then the other voice answered with an assumption of casualness, under which it trembled audibly: "I thought you said you were ready to back your opinion?"

"I am. Right; I'll take you. After all, there are plenty of girls about, aren't there, friend?" There was an unpleasant mocking jocularity in the last sentence, but the other disregarded it, saying in a low tone:

"No S.J. business, now. Loser to go right off and leave the winner an open field."

"Beloved son, have you ever heard that I didn't pay my debts of honour? I lost myself for a month once to Dick Watlay and obeyed him like a lamb, even when he made me enter for a course

in higher mathematics. I haven't got them off my stomach yet…
You'll get Molly all right, if you win her. That is, of course, if she'll
take you—after me."

The affected laugh sounded again. "Don't get angry. I daresay
she will. Why, that girl…" The voice sank to a furtive whisper.

They were over the sea now. Agatha Wayland, beside him, was
continuing an intermittent monologue about her son Terry, who
was to join them when the race was over.

"I wish his father would take more interest in him," she was
saying plaintively. "He hasn't taken any notice of him since Terry
said he wouldn't go to the university. Of course, it disappointed
him, when he is so clever; but then there are different kinds of
cleverness, aren't there? One of my uncles was a genius at making
pictures out of fish-bones. You wouldn't believe how pretty they
were. But they would never let him have an exhibition. Everyone
said what a shame it was… Fish-bones are such awkward, slippery
things, too. I'm glad they always take them out now. Ena had one
stuck in her throat once when she was little; the surgeon had to
come and get it out… Everyone can't go to the university, can
they? There was that time they tried it—my mother was a young
girl then—she was one of those that had nervous break-downs.
But Terry is clever enough in his own way, even if he doesn't care
about books. He's much better known than his father ever was or
is likely to be. Didn't you know they said he was the best English
racer that there has been for ten years? But Robert doesn't think
anything of all that. He wouldn't come to-day for anything I could
say. You might almost think he was jealous of the boy—but I suppose it can't be that." She paused to sigh. "Some of my friends
told me I was a fool to marry out of my class, and I suppose they
were right, only people didn't think so much about it then…"

Guy was absorbed by the approach of the French coast with the sun shining on its string of seaside towns. When he began to listen again, she appeared to be describing the finish of a former race in which Terry had taken part.

"When he came in he was falling down every minute—then he'd get up and drag himself a few steps and then fall down again. He was white as paper, and the sweat was dripping off him. They said the next racer was just coming over the rise; but I didn't see him. I cried, I did truly. I said I'd never see a finish again as long as I lived. You don't know what it is to a mother to see her boy like that. The people were nearly mad. They kept going back to him and then running on in front of him, trying to make him go quicker. But, of course, he couldn't, poor boy. And then he seemed to wake up a bit and looked round and saw the other man coming up behind him, and he gave a sort of cry and ran the last yard or two and dropped down, as if he were dead. They had three doctors to him in less than a minute, and the police had to drive the crowd off him with their sticks. But he didn't come round for half an hour. I was crying over him all the time, I was, indeed."

Something in the gusto of the description was faintly unpleasant to Guy. It came into his mind to ask her whether she approved of sporting contests which left a man in so abject a condition of exhaustion. But then it seemed an absurd question to put to Agatha Wayland.

It was almost noon when they drew near to their destination, a valley in the Swiss Alps at the foot of the mountain which had been chosen for the race.

Guy had heard no more of Agatha's conversation for the last half hour, as the great plane threaded its way, hardly slackening speed, around the shoulders of the great mountains, along the course of blue lakes, and up through narrow valleys with rushing rivers. He had no more appreciation of scenery than have most people; it usually required the dramatic to awaken his æsthetic sense; but these were his first mountains. Their white heads, rank behind rank, crowding around the horizon, fascinated him with an impression of unreality as if he were looking at an invented picture, at some strange, vast drop-scene in a titanic theatre. The steely, glittering, irregular patches here and there on their sides were like nothing he had ever seen or imagined, and yet he recognised them at once, thrilling, as glaciers.

A rushing grey river, springing out of one of these patches in a ravine far up the mountain, came down the middle of the valley where they landed, which expanded at this point into a green plain dotted with chalets. The number of people at present in it must have been immense, and still they seemed nothing but clusters of black dots, too scattered to affect its air of remote loneliness.

Agatha Wayland had been forbidden by her son to fly up for the finish to the mountain-top, around which aeroplanes danced like flies. Guy had caught himself wondering whether the insensible athlete had, after all, felt some of his mother's tears dripping on his face on that former occasion of which she had told him. Anyhow, she had promised to go to the hotel which was his headquarters, and to stay near it until the result was known. If Terry won, they were to hold there a party of celebration in the evening.

They came down gently in an open stretch before the hotel, alongside the row of sister planes, and a moment later the one that was next behind them dropped beside them. The passengers swarmed out and hurried towards the nearest group, shouting questions. The race had begun some hours earlier. Guy caught some of the remarks that were being tossed about.

"The Von led at the last stage, all going strong. They've hardly settled down yet."

"Sandy said he was going up the glacier. It's optional."

"They say he trained entirely on porridge."

Guy followed his companions across the turf towards the hotel. For the first time he heard about him the mysterious babble of foreign languages.

Cheers and shouting rang out suddenly, and following the pointing fingers he saw, far up the mountain-side, just above the pine forest which covered its lower slopes, a white flag with a red cross fluttering out.

"Terry leads! Terry leads!" The English cry predominated.

Guy seized his field-glasses. They brought the mountain very close. Just above the flag he made out a little brown figure with something gleaming on its back, toiling steadily up a rough track. A moment later it rounded a pimple on the mountain-side and disappeared. Almost at the same instant, another figure, taller and more darkly clad, appeared out of the trees, and a tartan flag ran up below the other.

They lunched early, made hungry by the strong air. Then Agatha Wayland was found by acquaintances, who seized upon her with shrill delight in discovering someone connected with the English hero. Guy wandered about alone for a time, and presently found himself unexpectedly suffering the boredom of the onlooker at a sport of which he knows nothing. It seemed a tiresome waste of opportunity to wait there watching for flags to flash out at long intervals up the mountain-side, or to follow the scrambles of the climbers, yard by yard, with field-glasses. He had already twice watched the start shown on an open-air stereomovie. Yet everywhere about were groups and couples talking and gesticulating excitedly. He began to suspect them of similar bargains to the one which he had overheard in the aeroplane, and which had left a faintly unpleasant taste in his mouth.

As always now, when a disagreeable impression threatened, his attention wandered away to something else. The novel countryside cried to him for exploration, and the stimulating air made him eager to be moving. He would get out of the crowd and wander away. But he was still restrained by a slight timidity in going about alone. He determined to rouse Ena, who was sitting listlessly by the wooden table at which they had lunched. She had not spoken to him yet; it was time, he thought, that the stupid embarrassment between them should be cut through.

He went up to her and proposed that they should climb to the top of a low ridge near at hand, from which there should be a clearer view of the mountain-side.

Ena looked up at him, startled. Then her eyes filled with tears. She sprang to her feet.

"I'll go anywhere," she declared vehemently.

Guy laughed a little, disconcerted by her emphasis, and took refuge in commonplace observations. "It won't take us more than an hour to get there… Your mother seems to be fixed up for the present. We shall be back before she wants us."

They started off gaily. Ena recovered her spirits instantly and began chattering away as usual. Guy, absorbed in the pleasure of exploring, listened to less than half of what she said. They soon began to draw out of the throng of spectators, and found a little track leading through the pine woods in the direction that they wanted to take.

Neither of them had any experience of climbing. When their little path led them, after a scramble, out of the woods and round a shoulder of the hill out of sight of the valley and then zigzagged down into an unexpected hollow, they thought that it would take them, perhaps, ten minutes longer than they had expected to reach the point at which they were aiming. The crisp air filled them with energy and eagerness. The little adventures of the path, which became rougher and rougher, kept them entertained. At one point they had to walk along the rock face for a few yards on a track about eighteen inches wide with a considerable drop below. Ena followed Guy without a moment's hesitation, and flushed with pleasure when he praised the steadiness of her head. He helped her to leap from stone to stone across the stream at the bottom of the hollow. They shouted with laughter when the last leap fell short and he had to pull her to the bank wet above the ankles. They were hungry again by this time, and sat down to share a cake of chocolate from Guy's pocket before attacking the farther slope.

This turned out to be more formidable than it looked. The ground was bare and stony, and the track led sometimes around large boulders, sometimes over them. It was a series of scrambles, making frequent pauses necessary. They were still far from the top when Guy suddenly felt a misgiving, suggested perhaps by the beginning of real fatigue in his untrained muscles. He pulled out his watch.

"Great Scott! Do you know what time it is?"

Ena shook her head, her eyes shining trustfully at him.

"It's after five. We must get back at once. The race will be almost over."

The journey back was more silent than the outward one. Guy was beginning to understand enough about mountaineering to reject Ena's suggestion that they might find a short cut by rounding the upper part of the dip. None the less, they missed their track and were obliged to cross the stream at a more difficult point. The sun had already sunk, for them, behind the opposite slope, but the ridge above them was still bathed in sunlight. Guy instinctively hurried his pace.

They were half-way up when he heard a smothered sob behind him. He turned round sharply. Ena had collapsed in a little heap by the path.

"Tired?" He spoke with cheery boldness in the effort to conceal his dismay. "We'll rest for a few minutes."

"I can't go on. I can't. I tried as long as I could. I did, Guy Martin; I did."

"Oh, nonsense!" said Guy briskly. "You're a little out of breath, that's all. You'll be all right in a minute."

"It's not that. It's my feet. Oh, Guy, they do hurt so."

"Let me see." Without ceremony Guy lifted the crumpled figure and placed her sitting against a boulder. He knelt to examine her feet.

The result appalled him. Her shoes had evidently been light ones with heels somewhat high. No doubt she had wanted to cut an elegant figure in her brother's circle; she was also wearing stockings for the first time since he had met her. One of the heels had now gone altogether. The thin leather of both shoes was cut into strips, and, through the gaps, Guy could see the raw, blistered flesh.

"Why on earth didn't you tell me?" he demanded furiously.

"I would never have told you—never. I said I would go till I dropped, and I did. I didn't keep you back."

Guy stared at her. In some incomprehensible manner the disaster seemed to her to be not that they were stranded here on the mountain-side with the night coming on, but that she had been compelled to betray her insufficiency to him.

He was irritated with himself, too, because he had not observed her plight sooner, and this made him speak the more sharply.

"I don't understand you. Any sensible person would know that you couldn't do rough walking in shoes like that."

Ena had begun to sob a little disconsolately. "It's all over. Now you'll go on and leave me, and never want to take me for a walk again."

The ridiculous, pitiful little speech dashed Guy's irritation with compassion. "Don't be absurd," he said more gently. "Of course I shan't leave you... That would be a nice thing to do, wouldn't it, after we have been such good pals all day? We must camp here for the present, and no doubt they will send people out to search for us."

He did not feel so sure of this as he pretended, and wondered whether, after all, he ought not to leave her and go for help. But remembering the long rough way they had come, he was beginning to feel doubtful of his own capacity to reach the hotel before dark. It seemed better to stay together and make the best of it. It appeared to him extremely unlikely that they would be found before the morning, and the prospect of a night on the hillside with a hopelessly lame companion loomed unpleasantly before him.

But Ena seemed to have no such misgivings. She had stopped crying at his assurance and sat up. "They'll have all the aeroplanes out in an hour or two," she said carelessly. Then eagerly again: "What is a pal? Would you leave me if I were a man, Guy?"

Guy was irritated afresh by the question. "No, of course I shouldn't," he said curtly. He laid hands, not too gently, on one of her shoes, saying: "We must get these off at once."

Ena turned white, but made no sound.

Guy clenched his teeth, and, using his pocket knife, presently managed to remove the remnants of the dainty shoes. She leaned back against the boulder while he did it, pale, with closed eyes. But he could not bring himself to tear the shreds of stockings away from the raw patches.

"Listen, Ena," he said a little sternly, because he was so sorry for her. "I can't get these away without water. I shall have to go back to the stream for some. I shan't be long."

He was longer than he expected. The only thing he had in which he could carry water was one of his own boots, and he was obliged to tear up his shirt into strips to bind round the unshod feet, as he climbed painfully back. It was becoming dark by the time that he reached Ena again. She was looking out wildly, and gave an hysterical cry as he loomed up out of the dusk.

"Oh, Guy, you've been such a long time. I thought something dreadful must have happened." She seized his arm feverishly.

Guy abruptly disengaged himself. "Don't upset it, for Heaven's sake, after I've brought it all this way," he exclaimed.

"I'm sorry," Ena whimpered. "I thought you'd fallen over a precipice. I knew you wouldn't go away. You said you'd never desert a pal, didn't you?"

"We've got to get this done before it's too dark." Guy tore a fresh strip from the remnant of his shift.

"You've brought it in your boot—your own boot—for me." Ena seemed to find something profoundly moving in the fact.

"Nothing else to bring it in," said Guy, deliberately matter-of-fact. She was extraordinarily difficult to deal with, this child-woman. She seemed to have no sense at all of the practical exigencies of their situation, but only of some emotional absurdities intangible to anyone but herself.

He began his surgeon's work with as little clumsiness as possible, remembering with a grim smile certain route marches during the short period of military training which he had once undergone. Ena leaned back again, very pale, closing her eyes. He wished she would help him, but it was natural that she should be feeling sick. Her feet were really in a very nasty state, though, of course, the damage appeared much less as soon as the bad places had been washed, even as inadequately as he was able to do it. At least, she gave no trouble over it, letting him do as he pleased without a wince or a moan.

At last he had tied the remaining shreds of his shirt around the damaged feet. They looked like shapeless bundles of rag, but he was proud of his handiwork, as man is always.

"There," he said, and proceeded to empty and painfully replace his own soaked boot on his swelling foot. "You've been very brave. Isn't that more comfortable?"

"It's divine." Ena's eyes opened, and smiled at him. The absurd adjective embarrassed Guy, but he was obliged to smile back to the appeal of her smile.

She sighed contentedly. "I don't mind them in the least now. I think this is beautiful. I wish it would go on for ever. But I expect the aeroplanes will come soon."

Guy thought, looking up at the blue sky, in which the stars were beginning to appear, that the sooner they came the better. It was becoming chilly, and he shivered. There was no shirt now under his tweed coat. Ena was shivering a little, too. He wondered if he ought to take off his coat and wrap it around her, but his chivalry was unequal to the sacrifice of exposing his naked chest and back to the bite of the night air. The unadmitted idea at the back of his mind was that he would like to offer and be refused, but he could not be sure that she would refuse if he did offer. He could never be sure what she would do or say under any given circumstances.

Meanwhile the girl was going on, dreamily: "It's like a scene out of an old novel. You and I lost on the mountain-side with the night coming on, and you saving my life like that."

"I haven't saved your life," said Guy hastily. "Look here, it's getting too cold to stay in this open place. I think I'll look round and see if I can find anywhere more sheltered. I won't go out of call."

He moved off at once without waiting for her to answer.

The hillside was the most forbidding place for a camp that he could have imagined, but there were big boulders here and there which might offer a slight shelter from the wind. He found presently a little hollow on the leeward side of one of them, and went back to fetch his companion, bracing himself groaningly for the effort of carrying her. But just as he reached her, a great sound broke the stillness.

It was stupefying. It was like the last trump rending the darkness; it was as if St. Michael were calling his army of gods to the battle of Armageddon. Guy stood, stricken motionless. The immense voice was forming articulate words:

"Ena Wayland and Guy Martin, or anyone knowing whereabouts, please answer. Searchers out... *On cherche* Ena Wayland *et* Guy Martin. *Répondez qui pouvez.*" Then words in a language unknown to him, repeating the names.

"Guy!" Ena's whisper came to him shrilly across the gap between them. Instinctively he moved closer to her, and she seized his arm eagerly. "Shall we keep quiet for a little longer?" There was an urgent appeal in the whispered words. "They'll come back again later. Let us wait."

Guy recovered his presence of mind. "Of course not." He turned on her. "Tell me quickly how to answer."

"You've only to shout," she answered, sulkily, after a moment. "They will have an amplifier."

The great voice sounded again up in the darkness, a little farther off, repeating its formula. As soon as it ceased, Guy shouted at the top of his voice:

"Here! We're here!" His efforts sounded like an insect answering the thunder. "They'll never find us by that," he said to Ena.

"Won't they?" She laughed resentfully.

The great voice, seeming to fill the whole horizon, and nearing like a rising gale, addressed them conversationally.

"Very good. We have your position. We shall reach you in five minutes."

Guy was silent, full of wonder; the story of Job, read to him in a child's version long ago, came into his mind. He had always imagined the voice of God coming out of the sky like this. The marvels of this new world were inexhaustible.

A few moments later a shaft of light began to play over the valley, and almost instantly they were bathed in its white radiance. Looking upwards, they saw at the apex of the light-fountain a hovering aeroplane, which sank slowly towards them. And now, at last, there was audible the faint purr of the engine.

"We can't land there," called someone, leaning over the side. "We'll let down a ladder to you. No one injured, is there?"

Guy called back cheerfully that they could manage to climb the ladder.

His relief was intense. His responsibility for the rash expedition had been weighing on him even more heavily than fatigue. In the reaction, he realised suddenly how foolish he had been to suppose that one could fall into serious trouble in this wonderfully ordered new civilisation with its endless resources. It would seek you out and save you in any imaginable scrape. It was practically foolproof. He understood that Ena had been perfectly justified in not taking their predicament seriously. Child of the new times, she knew that her civilisation was all-pervading and would watch over her as well on an Alpine mountain-side as in the middle of London, and that she could afford to indulge her odd impulses here as well as anywhere. He helped her, squealing a little now with the pain of those unnecessary blisters, up the light metal staircase into the plane. As they entered the warm, lighted saloon, the adventure shrank to the ridiculous incident of an afternoon.

The stout young man who came forward, grinning, to meet them, seemed to know Ena.

"Well, here's a handsome show, Ena Wayland. I can tell you the champion is raging that his sister wasn't there to meet him."

"He's won? Terry's won?" Ena clasped his arm dramatically. It seemed as if her whole being hung upon his answer.

"A walk-over. Everyone is *loco*. The Von was seventeen minutes behind. I didn't hear about the rest. Terry sent half a dozen of us questing for you as soon as he knew you were missing."

Ena drew up her small figure. "You must take me at once to my brother's headquarters," she said.

The young man guffawed. "Seeing that's what I've been sent for, I should take you if I had to drag you," he said.

Ena turned her back on him and walked to a mirror in the wall, where she stood patting and preening herself like a small bird at its toilet.

"Oh, that's Guy Martin," she said carelessly, over her shoulder.

Guy felt himself redden at the tone. The sudden visible change from childish dependence to childish vanity irritated him, even while he felt it foolish to be annoyed at the vagaries of a being so irresponsible. He turned to the man and asked brusquely if he had any food, then went over to the window with the plate of sandwiches that was produced. The stout young man further exasperated him by letting his gaze move slowly and grinningly from Ena to himself and then winking at him.

"Well, I've got to tell them you're found." He moved off and ostentatiously left them. After a moment Ena glanced round.

"I'll ask Terry to take you about with him if you like," she volunteered.

"Thanks. Don't trouble," said Guy shortly.

"It's no good trying to make yourself look as if you had been strolling down the boulevards. It can't be done," he added a moment later with schoolboy brutality, and was immediately angry with himself for doing so.

They finished the journey in silence.

Almost at once the plane entered a great glare of light which filled half the valley with an artificial day, throwing the dark forms of the mountains into eerie relief. The sky above them was lit up with fiery portraits and inscriptions. On the ground were swarming crowds of little figures. Stereomovie films were showing everywhere to cheering audiences. Around the hotel itself was a huge compact crowd only kept from blocking the main entrance by a band of men in uniform. At intervals a series of roars for "Terry Wayland" would break from it.

The young man offered Ena his arm as they climbed out of the plane and led her quickly towards the entrance. Guy followed behind with the irritated sensation of being in tow, like a dog on a lead. Ena had slipped on a long aeronaut's cloak, which hid her dishevelled tunic and bandaged feet; and Guy, knowing the anguish it must cost her, could not help admiring her for walking without a limp.

She was recognised as they entered and cheers given for Terry's sister. She dropped her escort's arm and turned round in the doorway, her little dark face wreathed in smiles, evidently prepared to make some actress's response. It was impossible for Guy to get out of the way in time. She stumbled over him; his impetus carried them across the threshold, and the moment was gone.

Ena gripped his arm viciously as she recovered her balance.

"I hate you!" she threw out at him.

And Guy, looking down into her face, saw that, for the moment at least, the statement was true.

III

Blaring noise and light held Guy still for a moment in the doorway of the room in which Terry Wayland was holding his celebration, and to which their guide had hurried them. He had a confused vision of numbers of people eating, drinking, talking, gesticulating, strolling about restlessly. As a background to the confused gabble came the rumble of the crowd outside, heard through an open window, and rising now and then in a series of systematic shouts.

The room in itself was bewildering. Old-fashioned wooden walls, with the heavy fixed seats of an ancient inn parlour, contrasted queerly with a superimposed profusion of lounge-chairs, rugs, cushions, divans, luxurious and brightly coloured as in an Eastern palace, so that the whole gave the almost indecent effect of an old woman in gay clothes. In the centre of the room, on a great divan, a sturdily built youth in a gorgeous dressing-gown rested against a pile of cushions, while a young man at the foot of the couch massaged one of his tremendous calves. Guy looked

curiously at him. He had a broad, heavy face, of sallow complex-
ion, surrounded by close dark curls; and Guy perceived immediately how, with the curious sameness in difference of family
likenesses, Agatha Wayland's features underlay his. The scene
suggested vaguely a kind of court—bringing back a shadowy
recollection of something seen long ago, perhaps in one of the
cinematograph films of old Roman life, which had been popular
in the early twentieth century—of some burly young gladiator-
emperor lying in the midst of his satellites. People in the far corners
of the room were talking and laughing among themselves, but
there was a constant polarisation towards the divan, and, when
the young man who lay on it spoke, everyone stopped to listen.

Ena had darted forward instantly to her brother's side, and
dropped on her knees, with a dramatic cry:

"Oh, Terry! Terry!"

"Oh yes, I daresay." The young athlete turned to look at her, his
lips curling unpleasantly. "You've been thinking of nothing but me
all the time, haven't you?… You couldn't even be here to welcome
me back. Where have you been, I want to know? And who is that
with you?… Shut those maniacs up, if you can, George Brady."

A man went over to the window and leaned out.

"Don't be angry, Terry," Ena pleaded, her head coaxingly on
one side. "We only went for a short little walk up the mountain-
side—just to get a better view of the race. And then I hurt my foot
and we couldn't get back… And it's only Guy Martin."

"Oh, is it?" Terry just brushed Guy with his eyes. "Well, you'll
please remember another time that I like my family to be there
when I come back from a race… By God, Sam Dowler," he turned
viciously on the masseur, "if you can't do better than that, I'll never
let you touch me again."

The masseur cringed, muttered abject apologies, and went on with his work with fingers that trembled visibly.

The clamour outside became shot suddenly with shriller, more irregular cries.

"They're fighting for your souvenirs," said the man called George Brady, from the window. The voice struck Guy's ears familiarly, and the next moment he remembered that it was that of one of the men whose strange bet he had overheard in the aeroplane that morning—the one who had staked on Terry's victory. He examined him with interest. He was a little dark man— somehow, Guy had known that he was small, although he had never glanced round—with deep-set eyes that smouldered with excitement.

Terry swore at the crowds for fools, while pleased grins ran one after another across his face. The psychological weather in the room changed abruptly; laughing and talking broke out again. Terry aimed a playful kick at the masseur's face, and laughed at his astonished expression as he sprawled on the floor.

"Sam, you fool, you might as well try to massage with sticks of putty... There! It's hurt me quite as much as you. Stop it for to-night and go get a drink."

He had kept one heavy hand gripping Ena's shoulder, and now, with a flick, jerked her to her feet, turning her so as to face him.

"So you tried a taste of mountaineering, too?" he began to chaff her with a loud joviality. "Ha, ha, ha! I hope you enjoyed it? Let's see the state of your feet." He made a clumsy snatch at her cloak. She evaded him, giggling. All the room echoed with guffaws and giggles.

"Ha, ha, ha, you mountaineering!" The racer heaved with titanic fits of laughter. "That's too good. D'you hear that, George?

Never been on a mountain in her life—sets off with a man who has never been on a mountain in his life... You haven't, have you? Here, where are you?" He discovered Guy through the crowd, which hastened to clear an avenue between them, and regarded him waggishly. Guy shook his head. "I could tell that by the look of you. Ha, ha, ha!... Well, take him and make him drink... Everyone's got to be drunk to-night." Guy was boisterously seized and bundled into a chair by a table that was immediately covered with miscellaneous bottles.

"And then she thinks she'll be back in time for tea," Terry went on with his slow gibing. He glanced round at the company as if inviting them to follow his demonstration. "And that's what she's doing while the last stage of the International Race is running!"

The others joined in: "She means to be the next champion."

"Your mother's ready to spank you, Ena Wayland, when she comes back," from a shrill female voice.

"Lucky the man, anyhow. Perhaps he knows more than we think."

Ena, twisting under the fire of chaff, glanced momentarily in Guy's direction, but he would not respond.

Terry was saying ponderously, "That's a compliment, Ena. You'll have to kiss Tom for that." He emphasised his instructions with a resounding slap across the hips, bringing shouts of delight from the bystanders.

Ena shrieked and tottered away, crying: "Oh, you horror, Terry! I can't run! I can't run!"

The man who had spoken, egged on by his neighbours, took up the chase, which, in spite of Ena's lameness, went all round the room, with a series of stumbles and collisions which formed new centres for horseplay and laughter.

Guy drew back as close to the wall as he could, glad that he was forgotten in the new diversion. This broad, physical jocularity took him by surprise. He could not help feeling the disdain, combined with nervous alarm, natural to a sober man in the company of those who are slightly drunk, as he suspected Terry and most of his guests of being, and as Ena seemed very ready to be. And at the same time he felt a disinclination to join them by attaining a similar condition.

The young man at the window turned again suddenly and called into the midst of the riot:

"Be quiet a moment. There's something I can't make out. News of some sort, I think."

From the groups near to him spread a widening circle of silence through the room, and there gradually became audible another change in the note of the crowd outside—the difference between many people saying the same thing and many people saying different things.

Terry sat up straight on his couch, making a grimace of pain at the sudden strain on his stiffening muscles. The bystanders noticed it, and a curious, half-sympathetic, half-pleased grin momentarily passed over their faces.

"See what it is," the racer directed curtly.

There was some bustle at the door. A man came back with eyes that shone in a face set to solemnity.

"It's about Sandy," he said. "He fell down a crevasse. Broken his collar-bone and two ribs. They have got him into a Red Cross plane."

The room buzzed with talk. In two minutes all sorts of additions and variations were current, coming from no one knew where.

"Poor devil!"

"So his porridge hasn't done much for him, after all."

"Painful business that!" The speaker, who was standing near to Guy, screwed up his face, and a half-smile played about his lips.

Someone else, hustling up to the group importantly, threw out in a loud, husky whisper, thrusting his head forward: "He couldn't speak. One rib has pierced a lung. He keeps spitting blood."

A queer, undefined, sinister impression was overcoming Guy. The animation in the room was greater than ever, faces were more flushed, talking was momentarily quieter, but more eager; laughter on a more abandoned note was beginning to burst out. He no longer felt that it was one of the vulgar, uproarious parties which he had sometimes experienced among his own class in his former life, although they had never been much to his taste, but something different, with elements which he did not care to look at closely. He glanced at Terry Wayland through a gap in the crowd, and saw the victorious racer leaning back again against his cushions, silent for the moment, on his face a faint smile. Ena was not in sight. He experienced an instant of nausea, which he was able to suppress promptly. Then he understood suddenly that he was completely worn out and sick of impressions. That was what was wrong. It had been an exhausting day; his nerves were on edge. He began to make his way slowly and unobtrusively towards the door.

In the passage he stood still for a moment with a singing head. Some obscure sense of something left undone, some tiresome duty that should be attended to before he could rest, troubled him. Then he realised that it was nothing but a vague scruple against leaving Ena behind in those surroundings. But it did not delay him long. Ena was quite happy, and, anyhow, it was her mother's business to look after her. And, even while he thought it, he felt a conviction that, somewhere also, Agatha Wayland was the centre of a crowded roomful of admiring cronies. But no one could expect him, spent, and a stranger, to supply her deficiencies.

He made his way to a little bedroom very high up at the back of the house, far from the noise, and scribbled his name on the tablet outside. By the time he had pulled off his boots, he was staggering with sleep. He threw himself down on to the bed without undressing, drew the coverlets over him, and lost consciousness almost in the same instant.

IV

Guy awoke with an impression of very early morning, although it was already fully light; this was followed immediately by a sense of outrage, which was forthwith explained by the sound of a soft urgent knocking at his door.

He lay still for a moment, hoping that it would stop; then, as it only became more importunate and someone tried the handle, he sulkily climbed out of bed and went to open the door. He must unconsciously have locked it the night before as he took refuge from the racer's celebration.

Ena Wayland stood outside, fully dressed, her little dark face working with excitement.

"Oh, Guy! You wouldn't wake. Why did you lock the door? Come along quick!… There isn't a moment to lose. Listen! you can hear them. They'll be up here in a moment."

There was, in fact, the sound of a distant disturbance, many voices, and the slamming of doors.

"What are you talking about?" he demanded roughly, still regretting the sweet, dreamless sleep which lingered in his brain as a delicious flavour lingers on the palate.

"Oh, why are you so stupid?" She danced with impatience. "They're after you. I'm trying to get you away before they come. There are aerocycles out on the roof. If you'll only come at once!"

"After me!" exclaimed Guy incredulously.

"Yes. They'll smother you if they get you," she forced herself to stand still and explain with a desperate deliberation, glancing every second along the passage. "They will, truly. They're madly excited... It has come out that you are here. The police couldn't keep them back."

It dawned on Guy's sleepy senses with a thrill of horrified disgust that he was actually in some danger. There was no mistaking the genuineness of the girl's anxiety. It was not just some absurd whim of hers, as he had been ready to think. He let her seize his arm, and hurried beside her along the passage, pale and perspiring.

"Where are we going?" he muttered.

"Up here." She loosed hold of him and began to scramble up a narrow staircase leading to the door on to the roof. Guy followed her closely. The confused noise was coming nearer, and, as he reached the top of the staircase, the lift doors in the passage shot suddenly open, letting out a tumbling crowd of men and women. They caught sight of him as he disappeared, and raised a howling cry. He slipped through the door, slammed it behind him, shivering, and drove home a bolt. A row of aerocycles were stacked on a flat extent of stone. Ena had run to the nearest one and was already in the driver's seat, signalling to him to climb into the little side-seat, in which a passenger was sometimes carried. She began to screw her power-box into place, calling to him to

hold on tight. Just as he seated himself there came a battering at
the door behind them.

The next instant they shot up vertically with a stupefying veloc-
ity. Guy gasped and held his breath, expecting the stop immediately,
as in the upspring of a lift; but they rose and rose without respite.
It was like an endless plunge into icy water. A band seemed to
tighten around his head. He began to breathe again in great gasps,
holding desperately to the sides of his seat. Then, as the sensation
was becoming intolerable, they began to slow down, and presently
stopped dead. They were hovering above the morning haze, which
lay like a gauze veil over the earth beneath them, broken by the
shoulders of the mountains. The cold seemed to cut through
clothes and flesh to the bone.

He turned tremulously to Ena to speak, and at the same
moment, with faint humming noises, some half-dozen machines
sprang out of the mist, splaying in a circle around them. Ena
gave an exclamation, pressed down a lever, and they dropped
back again.

It seemed to Guy that it must have been half an hour at least
while they danced, wheeled, and dodged through the thin vapour.
Every time they approached clearer air they would catch sight of
some waiting plane and dodge back again. In the mist they could
see only a few yards, but now and then would come the near hum
of an engine, and a vague shape would loom near them, ghost-like,
or, more strangely still, a black wing would stick suddenly out of
a denser nucleus of vapour, like the fin of a shark at sea. Always,
at these moments, there would come a queer backward jerk of
their own plane, which puzzled Guy, until he remembered that
these planes became mutually repellent as soon as they rose into
the air. No doubt they owed it to this device that they escaped

collision. The knowledge that his enemies could not, at any rate, get to very close quarters while he remained in the air, reassured him a little.

Then, at last, after they had rested still for some moments, without hearing or seeing anything, Ena put over the lifting lever again, and they rose clear. There was nothing in sight.

"They've given us up," Ena laughed triumphantly.

Throughout the chase they had spoken only in whispered exclamations. Now, as they began to descend at a long slant, she was chattering gaily.

"They couldn't have got us, of course. But I didn't want them following us all the way to England. Don't you think I'm rather good at hide and seek? I haven't played for a long time… It will be all right to go down again now."

Guy was incapable of answering. He felt sick and giddy. He was still holding on to the framework of his seat. These flimsy little planes actually gave one a sensation of suspension and strained balance which was quite absent in the Leviathans. The rapid evolutions, combined with the dread of being caught, had shaken his nerve badly.

Ena was examining a diagram-map on a stand in front of her. It was dotted with the names of places, and furnished with a hand like a clock. She twisted this until it pointed in a north-westerly direction, to where London was marked on the outer rim. The aeroplane veered slightly to the left and began to move horizontally at an easy pace. They were sailing at a comfortable height down the broad Alpine valley. The sun was rapidly clearing the morning mists, which had stood them in such good stead, and began to pour a grateful warmth on their shivering bodies.

Guy's confidence began to return.

"Why," he said. His voice came hoarsely and he stopped to moisten his lips. "Why did they want to kill me?"

"To kill you? To kill you?" Ena turned and looked at him with wide eyes. "What are you talking about?"

"You said they were after me."

"Oh yes. But they didn't want to kill you. What an idea! They wanted to see you. But they would have half-killed you, I know. They caught Terry once, and they shook his hands and prodded his muscles until he was nearly dead. He couldn't move without groaning for weeks. That is why there were so many police about yesterday."

"But why me? Why me?" Guy urged desperately.

Ena looked at him in surprise. "You see, someone told them that the twentieth-century man was there. So naturally they wanted to see you."

Guy drew a quick breath. It was a relief and shock combined. The horror of being hunted for his life without any reason vanished, but a new insecurity took its place. No possibility of this kind had occurred to his imagination. He had grown into the habit of regarding himself as the favoured observer, almost a partner, in this new world; he had felt something almost like a proprietary sense in it. It was a devastating shock to realise that to the people he moved among he was, after all, nothing but a freak for show, to be stared at and prodded and man-handled. For a moment he felt in all its starkness the old primitive horror of outlawry—the agony of the new schoolboy who finds himself wearing combinations when everyone else is wearing a shirt.

Ena was going on, oblivious of the effect of her words.

"I suppose it was Mother. She always lets things out." She giggled suddenly as at a recollection. "Terry was madly vexed. He thought they were coming for him at first. When he found it was for you, he got into bed again, and turned his back and wouldn't speak another word... I believe he would rather be treated again as he was before than have them wanting you instead... But I knew you were different. You would hate it... So I ran away and came for you." She glanced at him; there was a wistfulness, a naïve appeal for approbation in the last sentences.

Guy braced himself to answer her. It was impossible to regard Ena otherwise than as in some way dependent, as needing constantly to be directed, encouraged, or checked. Even after the wonderful exhibition of skill that she had just given, after the morning's adventure initiated and contrived by her, the same psychological situation re-established itself as soon as they began to talk. It was as though a sheep-dog came back to its master after a clever piece of work, with wagging tail, asking for approval. The master cannot withhold his response, whatever thoughts and troubles are seething in his own mind. These have nothing to do with the dog, which, in elementary good faith, he must meet on its own plane.

Some such instinctive obligation acted on Guy, as Ena's eyes searched his face. And the very necessity was in some degree restorative, for it represented a real relationship in this world which was threatening to become alien.

"You were quite right," he smiled at her; then shivered a little, remembering the cry of the human pack as they had caught sight of him disappearing up the staircase. "It would have been horrible. It was very good of you to come and rescue me."

She looked at him with the shining of tears in her eyes.

"Was it what a good pal would do?" she asked.

The question disconcerted Guy, but he forced himself to respond heartily. His consciousness of what she had done for him grew uncomfortably strong, as his self-preoccupation faded.

"But you must be dreadfully tired?" he suggested. "What about your feet?"

"I'm not tired. I came away from the fête last night soon after you did." She brought out the statement so quickly as to give him an impression that she had been looking for an opportunity to introduce it—an impression reinforced by her quick, furtive glance at him. He made no comment. "Terry's trainer gave me some very good lotion for my feet," she pushed on, her voice trembling slightly. "They are much better."

"That's good!" Guy put warm good-will into his tones.

She glanced at him happily, then obviously suppressed some speech that was rising to her lips. Instead, she suggested a moment later that they should go down and look for a place for breakfast.

Guy found that he was faint with hunger.

They discovered a little mountain-inn still primitive enough for the broad, flaxen, maid-of-all-work to be already up and about her work. Neither of them spoke French with any fluency, or German at all, and there was much laughter and ingenuity over the provision of their hot coffee and stale bread. Their spirits rose like larks as they ate. Guy praised Ena's cleverness of the morning and her skill in manœuvring the aerocycle. She glowed with pleasure and began to describe eagerly the incidents of the early morning—the attack of the crowd on the front of the hotel, which she had seen from her window, her own escape up the backstairs, her frantic search for his room, and desperation when she could not make him hear. He had never seen her so natural and candid. There were no more of the sudden sentimental demands which so acutely disconcerted him. They lingered a long time over their breakfast, then despatched a message to Agatha Wayland, and set out again for England.

CHAPTER VIII

EUTHANASIA

I

WITH GUY'S COUNTRY EXPEDITION IN THE COMPANY OF John Wayland, not quite a week after the Mountain Race, began the second phase of his sojourn in the new age. But he understood later how the incidents of the intervening days had also had their part in preparing it.

In those days John had no share, for he passed them with Sylvia Grant in Scotland, and for the first time Guy found himself alone with the Wayland family in its entirety.

John had been there, however, at the moment of their return from the race, when they had come upon him and his uncle lunching late together in the garden.

Guy remembered afterwards the pleasantness of that return—the light drop of the aerocycle into the quiet garden where the two men were sitting tranquilly at the little white-clothed table. After the fever of the race, the red, grimacing faces and clamorous voices, and the excitement of his escape, there was a delicious refreshment in their tranquillity, in their quiet tones and confident eyes. They looked a little fatigued, both of them, he noticed, but with a colour of satisfaction, as if they had just accomplished an arduous bit of work. He was not surprised when Dr. Wayland mentioned that John had been helping him all the morning with an experiment in the laboratory.

John laughed at the description. "You mean to say, watching you make it."

"Providing me with what I needed, anyhow." Dr. Wayland rested his hand for a second on his nephew's shoulder.

The little action gave Guy a momentary twinge of loneliness. The two men seemed so much akin. Their physical likeness underlay the contrast between the settled wisdom of the older face and the intelligent vigour of the younger; but stronger still was the effect of spiritual affinity, a clear-cut refinement of manner and expression. Guy felt, before them, mentally clumsy and impeded, a spiritual clodhopper. He half turned to Ena for support, but his gay companion of the morning had become abashed and childish again as soon as she found herself in the presence of her father and cousin. She was sliding away awkwardly, and soon vanished, muttering some excuse.

Then Dr. Wayland began to talk to him with a calm friendliness, and the feeling of isolation left him. They listened interestedly to his account of the race and what had followed it. Curiously, the conversation did not bring back the panic which Guy had felt that morning on first realising himself as a hunted monstrosity. In this company the sense of his uniqueness was no longer oppressive. It seemed accidental and unimportant, having no connection with his essential personality. The eccentricity was in his pursuers.

"These normals," John smiled tolerantly, as Guy walked with him to the gate, "never miss a chance to get excited."

John was in his gayest mood. They gripped hands at parting, and John promised to resume Guy's interrupted education as soon as he came back. Guy guessed that the critical question of marriage or not was to be finally settled during this expedition.

II

Terry Wayland returned from the race with his mother for a short stay at home; and as the addition of a single new element will alter the whole nature of a chemical compound, the household altered into something quite other than it had been during Guy's first weeks in it. In the first place, Terry took up a great deal of room. To Guy there was something almost a little shocking in the mountain racer's superb physical development, his great limbs and masses of muscle. Although nowhere on Terry was there half an ounce of superfluous fat, he inevitably recalled to Guy one of the huge prize pigs fattened for show which he had been used to see at country fairs in his boyhood.

The big fellow was no longer, in his own home, the truculent bully that had dominated the party in the Swiss hotel. On the contrary, there was something almost pathetic about him. In spite of his light and wonderfully balanced tread, he succeeded in giving the effect of lumbering aimlessly about the house, like a Newfoundland dog confined to a small flat. His only solaces appeared to be the occasions when someone recognised him, and in evening revels with his friends, from which he would return the following morning with all the symptoms of a splitting headache. Guy thought once that he was about to invite his company to one of these—and it was possible to watch an idea dawning in Terry Wayland's face long before he became conscious of it himself— but he thought better of it in the end, probably remembering the diversion of public interest that had occurred at their first meeting.

Otherwise, he appeared to have forgiven Guy. In fact, he obviously took him into favour in order to make use of him as a confidant. The process was too naïve to be resented, as innocuous as the cupboard love of an animal. The necessity for it arose from a suppressed feud between Terry and his father in regard to Terry's future occupation. Terry himself intended to enter as a General Labourer—a class who did odd menial jobs for which it was still more convenient to use unskilled human labour than to bring machinery to bear. This kind of work was constantly decreasing, so that the supply of labourers was always in excess of the demand; the hours were absurdly short, and it was possible to get leave at almost any time. In this trade, Terry would be able to continue his career as a racer without hindrance. Dr. Wayland, on the other hand, was understood to wish that, although his son was unfit for any intellectual work, he should at least apprentice himself to a skilled trade.

Agatha Wayland, in accordance with all precedent, was on the side of her son. Neither of them, however, ever brought the question into the open with the Doctor, at any rate, in Guy's hearing. Both her long rambling arguments and his surly grumbles were invariably addressed to a third person. From the Doctor himself Guy never heard a word on the subject. Indeed, the Doctor was more and more frequently absent, and Guy never discovered when he expressed the opinions attributed to him by his wife and son. He sometimes wondered whether he had actually ever expressed any opinion at all, beyond a silent disdain.

His own tendency was to dismiss Terry as an ill-conditioned cub whom the new world had not yet had time to lick into shape—in other words, to regard him, but without the softening due to difference in sex, much as he regarded Ena. But, in spite of himself, he could not always keep an attitude of complete aloofness from the confused repinings of the mountain racer. They were so artless and so rudimentarily human.

"What does he want me to do?" Terry would demand, setting his heavy brow in a frown. "I'd have been a doctor like him if I could. It isn't my fault that I haven't got brains. There's only one thing I can do, and that is mountain racing; and that is just what he wants me to stop doing. I should like to know how he would like it if someone wanted to stop him dabbling in that laboratory of his... Of course, I know he thinks racing is no use to anybody, but I don't see what that matters. It isn't as if people were wanted. Everyone knows that all the trades are overcrowded—they'll have to reduce the labour period soon... So why should I go when there are people who can't do anything else, and when everyone wants me to go on racing? I should just be hanging round at the depots, and they'd never take the trouble to teach me anything, because the others would learn so much more quickly... If they were short of people it would be different; I'd go at once then and be glad to..." An unmistakable heartiness came into his voice as the idea of a real need for his services suggested itself, and Guy's respect for him involuntarily rose.

But the plaintive note was back again as Terry pursued his monologue on another tack. "I don't see how you can say that a thing is no use when it amuses people. It does do that, you know—well, you saw for yourself. Just as much as any actor or story-writer of the lot of them... And it isn't as if I meant to sponge on other people for my living, though there are plenty that would be glad to keep me. But I wouldn't have that. I shall get my coupons and power-boxes like everyone else, and I shall be there to work if I am wanted.—They'll have that on the stereos, you know: 'Terry Wayland begins his Work Period at the General Labourers' Depot.'... I think he might try to look at it from my point of view. Of course, he doesn't care about sport; but other people do... It's too much to expect a man to stop doing the only thing he can do. I should—I should—begin going for people, out of sheer *ennui*"—the French word sounded quaintly in the midst of Terry's unpolished periods—"or get all wrong with the women or something, if I wasn't obliged to train for races and think and plan about them. And I can tell you it takes a lot of thinking out, too... If we can't afford to keep up our sport it seems to me a poor business. We might just as well be back in the twentieth century."

Guy started. Terry had evidently spoken without intention, although he now knew something of Guy's history. But it had flashed across Guy's mind that this problem of the lout's occupation might indeed have been simpler in the despised century from which he himself came. It was a case where conceivably the compulsion of the god "Money" might for once have had a beneficent influence. For, in some obscure manner, which Guy did not trouble to analyse, the very essence of the difficulty appeared to be that it lacked reality. It did not, in any practical sense, matter what Terry did. And yet it was impossible to regard Terry's solid body in any sense other than practical.

III

The same tirade, with minor variations in Agatha's complaining treble and Terry's grumbling bass, formed the undersong to Guy's real interest during these days of John's absence. This was the mastering of the aerocycle. Ena's exploits at the time of their escape from the Swiss valley had roused in him a schoolboy enthusiasm. She helped him with an eagerness which sometimes verged on tremulousness, and he was quickly learning to command a more perfect machine than any he had ever known. Its management was far more easily acquired than that of a twentieth-century bicycle. Nevertheless, the achievement increased his general confidence and independence out of all proportion to its difficulty. And this also, as he realised afterwards, had its influence on what came later.

It was on the last of these mornings that Guy had his first sight of a twenty-second century newspaper. He had not hitherto missed them, tacitly assuming that they no longer existed, but had been superseded by the stereos and tape machines. Now, he found that their apparent absence in the household had been due only to Dr. Wayland's distaste, and that the other members of the family read them in secret.

Ena ran out with it as he walked up and down the drive listening to Terry, with Terry's arm thrown affectionately over his shoulders—a demonstration which Guy would very willingly have spared.

She was incoherent with excitement, thrusting the paper at her brother with impatient little jerks, as he slowly pulled up and disengaged himself from Guy. Guy, accustomed by this time to discount Ena's excitements, waited, glancing curiously over Terry's shoulder. It seemed of small bulk, this newspaper of the new time (a fact, as he afterwards discovered, due chiefly to the absence of advertisements), and the page at which they were looking was headed strangely, in block letters of crimson,

"CRIMES PASSIONNELLES OF THE DAY"

The two Waylands began a jerking, unilluminating dialogue.

"It is, isn't it?" Ena was white and her eyes were glowing in a queer gloating manner. In spite of his scepticism, her expression roused in Guy a vague discomfort.

"Wait a moment; let me see." Terry took the paper in both hands and got down to the matter, his mind visibly passing through some process of unpleasant adjustment.

"There couldn't be two George Bradys," urged Ena.

"Oh God, no!" Terry groaned. "It is George all right... Poor devil... Here, read it to us."

Ena began to read:

> "No doubt who killed Molly Gatling, is there? Here's the story! Girl twenty-one, very pretty, and knows it too, so people say. Two lovers, Brian Travers, store official, tall, good-looking, pleasant, a cynical drawl, and 'a way with women'; George Brady, small, shy, insignificant, but devoted, very devoted—in fact, devotion the only remarkable thing about him. Travers has it all his own way up to about a week ago. Then, without warning, he stops coming. George still comes, though. Evidently expects a warmer welcome now, but certainly does not get it. Interested neighbours overhear vague sounds of recrimination. The usual chaff goes round.
>
> "Yesterday afternoon, Brady is seen to enter cottage while Molly is there alone—mother out paying a call. Molly is glimpsed at the window and never seen alive again. Mother, returning, gets a shock. Molly lying on

the floor—no longer pretty. In short, usual circumstances—torn clothing, finger-marks at throat, face
discoloured—"

"Oh God, stop that!" Terry growled. "Read what it says about
George."

Ena dragged reluctantly a moment, then passed on:

"An aerocycle is gone from the garden at the back.
Where? Well, one lands a few minutes later outside the
depot where Travers works. Quiet young man inquires
for him at the door. Was he trembling? Did his eyes
shine? Were there little drops of perspiration on his
forehead? The doorkeeper thinks so now. But he took no
count of it then… Travers is almost due to leave. Quiet
young man will wait outside. Five minutes. Quiet young
man walks up and down. Right hand in his pocket.
Looks up with a jerk when anyone comes out. Travers
at last. But he turns away sharply without noticing the
other. Quiet young man merely stands and stares. How
stupid! Is he going to let him go without speaking to
him, after all? But no! Quiet young man suddenly begins
to run after him, crouching a little, like a cat after a
mouse. Right hand comes out of his pocket. Something
gleams in it. But only for a moment. Before anyone can
interfere the gleam is hidden in Travers' body. A heavy
fall. Carried by his impetus, the young man rolls over his
victim, who falls with a gurgling groan, gives a twitch
or two, and then lies still. Very little blood. Bystanders
come to their senses; shouts, confusion. They are on

to the little man before he can get up. Police come and pull him out.

"A case for summary justice, obviously. Brady confesses the double crime. And so three more young lovers pay the ultimate tribute to the god they serve."

"And we were in the same room with him on Thursday!" Ena added in an awe-stricken whisper.

Terry swore deeply. "He'll never get off with two of them. If it had only been one—! I always knew he would go that way in the end."

To Guy a phrase spoken in light, mocking tones was repeating itself over and over in his brain: "If she'll take you after me! If she'll take you after me—after me!"

Then the horror came home to him with the peculiar vividness of personal contact. He knew that he had seen the beginning of it. It seemed a luridly fantastic touch that it should have happened on that morning when he had started out in such gay high spirits, so pleased with the life of the new world and trustful of its prevailing harmony. This was not the first time that he had come into contact with a crime of violence. There had once been an unpleasant case of murder and suicide in his native village. But he had supposed that things of that nature no longer occurred in this happy and enlightened time. Now, as his nerves struggled to readjust themselves, he told himself that he had been unreasonable. All the misery resulting from inequalities of wealth—immense and far-reaching as it was—had indeed gone, but it was too much to expect that there should be no occasional cases still of twisted minds and thwarted instincts. Even now, everything could not always be perfectly right for everyone.

Curiously enough, it was to the maddened little man himself, whose feverish, unsatisfied eyes he had noticed in that thronged room at the Swiss hotel, that his sympathy reached out, and not to his victims.

"Terry, was he madly in love with her?" Ena was questioning in an eager whisper.

"Oh, I suppose so. How the devil should I know?" Terry turned on her savagely. "I've something else to think about than girls—and a—good thing, too! There was a lot of talk about George and a girl who wouldn't have anything to do with him. He hasn't been himself for months. Confounded little cocotte! What did she think she was worth? They're the devil, women."

Ena shrank a little from his temper, but went on in an obsessed, furtive murmur, her eyes gleaming: "And she and the other man had been lovers, had they?"

Terry broke away with an oath, "—you, Ena! Can't you stop asking questions? It will all be in to-morrow's paper, you can bet your soul." He strode up the avenue away from them and took up his habitual position leaning over the gate.

"He needn't have been so cross," Ena muttered, looking after him. "I only wanted to know—"

A wave of distaste passed through Guy's body. "If you want to know," he said hastily, "I think your questions quite as disgusting as he does."

Ena gazed at him a moment, quite still, her brown eyes enlarging into a stare of dismay. Her little bunched figure incongruously reminded him of a rabbit "frozen" by terror. Then, as on the evening when she had announced her religious vocation, her face suddenly crumpled and collapsed. She turned and ran crouching towards the house in a welter of tears.

Guy faced about and followed Terry to the gate. It was Terry's favourite position, for sooner or later someone would be certain to pass who would recognise him for the celebrity he was; but, this time, Guy acquitted him of any afterthought. He put a hand on his shoulder and made an awkward attempt to express his sympathy. For the first time he almost liked Terry when he turned and said, with candid trouble in his voice: "Thanks, Martin. It's good of you. So many good fellows go that way—and now—George. He was only a little rat, you know—but, well—nice to have about."

But in another ten minutes he was back again, labouring round and round the treadmill of his own grievances.

IV

Guy watched John come up the avenue the next morning, humming to himself, wantonly switching at a flower with his stick now and again, and he felt his heart expand. John was so complete, so full of careless mastery, one could be so sure that he would never repeat himself. Terry had gone off the afternoon before and had not reappeared, and Ena had not come near him since the scene in the garden. Fresh society—John's society, gay and reassuring, came like the opening of a window in a stuffy room.

"You've missed me?" The remark was more statement than question, but John's quizzical smile redeemed its egotism.

"I have," Guy smiled back candidly.

"Ah!"

They had arranged to see the countryside that day, and took an automobile—a strangely shrunken and foreshortened automobile, suggesting absurdly to Guy a face without a nose. As they sped with a hardly perceptible hum along the swift traffic road out of town to the south, Guy told him of the occurrences of the previous day.

"I suppose he'll be convicted at the trial and sentenced to death?" he said.

"Probably done already," John told him perfunctorily. "We don't waste so much time over these matters as you used to, when there's no doubt about the facts."

"Then you still have capital punishment?" Guy shivered slightly.

"Yes." John was obviously preoccupied with something else, and the next moment he spoke out suddenly with a change of tone:

"Martin, I am going to risk offending you."

"I don't think you could do that," Guy laughed.

"Don't be sure until you hear what I have to say," John told him. "And don't forget that facts, and therefore views, have altered since the time when you acquired your modes of thinking. To put it straight to you, you should be careful in your dealings with my cousin Ena."

"What do you mean?" Guy had taken the preliminaries with a smile, but he sat up straight at the last sentence and jerked the words out.

"Ah," John sighed, throwing at him a half-amused, half-depre-catory glance. "I was afraid we might have another demonstration of 'proper pride.'... I wasn't sure. It is so difficult to know whether the psychological reactions in old plays and novels are genuine or were romantic conventions. You had so many of those. However, apparently this really hits the target."

"I merely want to know what you mean," Guy persisted coldly.

"This," said John. "You must realise that such matters have not stayed precisely where you left them, any more than has anything else. People have altered to match circumstances, and especially their development in youth takes a rather different course. That is admitted by all social psychologists. You see, we have no preoccupations with the business of getting a living, or of becoming or appearing richer than other people, which made the central interests of your lives; so, naturally, our minds concentrate all the more on other interests. And, with normals, those interests are chiefly emotional. For instance, they fall in love much more often and more enthusiastically than I imagine young men and women did in your day. It is almost a recognised psychological principle that a normal remains a child until he or she falls in love—in fact, it is not considered mentally safe for them to leave childish interests until that happens. With us, of course, it is different. We have things that interest us to learn. You may have noticed how much more childish Ena is than Sylvia, for instance—I think I saw you notice it?"

Guy murmured assent. He was still ruffled, but John's detached lucidity was beginning to dominate his mind as usual, though he struggled against it.

"Well, to come to the present case, it is perfectly obvious to any outside observer that you have become the means by which Ena is growing up. It is inconvenient for you, but it is much better that you should know it. And, since you are strange to our psychology, I think it only just to warn you that you must not expect any reserve from my aunt's family."

Involuntarily there flashed across Guy's mind the memory of an impression which he had never interpreted to himself, leaving it as a man can sometimes leave unacceptable ideas neglected in the outer fringe of his consciousness. It was the impression of Agatha Wayland's face as he and Ena came forward together to meet her when she came up the path, returning after them from the Mountain Race. He knew now of what it had reminded him. In the London of the twentieth century he had once been taken to a house in a back street by a "man of the world" fellow-clerk, and had visited it thereafter occasionally in his moments of physical urgency, to come away later, with empty pockets, sick, tired, and ashamed. It was bitten into his brain that, as the old woman of the house showed him into a room, the look of mingled obsequiousness and greed on her wrinkled face would give way to an indescribable expression, shot with a certain smirking delight. It was the dim counterpart of that look that had been on Agatha Wayland's broad, stupid face, as she saw her daughter and her guest advancing towards her across the lawn.

He pushed the obscene impression hastily down again and made a clutch at wholesome commonplaceness, summoning the atmosphere of all the plain, merry, open-air things of his life with the Waylands—the light freshness of his little room; the crisp rolls of his breakfast; the plunges into the half-shaded, half-sunny pool in the garden; the fun of his first clumsy efforts to guide the aerocycle, and Ena laughing at him; the sweet hay in the near-by fields which had just been mown a second time.

He was still irritated with Ena for her behaviour of the day before, but, as he remembered all the incidents and little adventures of their companionship, his instinct of loyalty revolted against this conversation. It seemed intolerable that she should be held up nakedly for inspection, played upon by the spot-light of John's cool logic.

"You are certainly mistaken," he said stiffly. "Your cousin has been kind to me as a guest; that is all. It is absurd to suggest that she has ever regarded me in any other light."

There was the sound of a stifled laugh from John.

"Beloved son," he said, "stop quoting your novelists. And don't suppose that I am blaming our poor Ena. She can't help it, any more than a pig can help grunting. Naturally, you are a romantic figure to her, dropping in suddenly as you did out of another century—though I doubt if she knows quite the whole truth about that—and just at the moment when her childish phase was becoming hopelessly outworn."

"You are wrong, and I wish you would drop the subject," Guy broke out boyishly.

"I will drop it certainly if you wish—vivid old phrase that—like a dog with a bone," said John, "especially as you recognise well enough that I am right… You must decide for yourself how you will deal with the matter."

They sat silent for a time, travelling at an easy pace through a countryside which Guy hardly recognised as the Kent of his boyhood. For it was all London: not the London of the old days, but the London of the new, spreading in groves and meadows and scattered buildings over whole shires. Kent had, indeed, become the garden of England; a garden specialised for pleasant living. Boundary walls and hedges had vanished; no black lines of railways cut across the greenness, but only stripes of white, dustless road. The houses—mansions, chalets, and cottages—stood each in a wide domain, like sailing-ships in a green sea whose tides swept un-stemmed right to the border of the road on each side of them. The interest of it and the pleasant motion soon soothed Guy's ruffled mood. He began to ask questions, and John responded with his imperturbable good-humour. They lunched in Canterbury, reduced to a small nucleus around the cathedral, which was almost as Guy remembered it, and came back by a circuit to the west, passing through the Surrey hills. This was an even more populous district, a hill-city extending from London, but with wide stretches of heath. Aeroplanes rose and flew over it in coveys; automobiles dashed along its double roads; but the red motor buses, which Guy remembered, scuttling over it like giant ladybirds, had vanished for ever.

V

Set back on a hillside, with acres of green park around it, they came upon what was evidently some important building, a gleaming white marble palace, with towers and domes, so lovely in the sunshine that Guy exclaimed and touched his companion's arm.

John reflected a moment before responding. "Come now," he said at last, smiling. "I won't tell you what that is yet, but we will get out and examine it, and afterwards, if you have not already guessed, I will explain it to you."

He drew up near the white-pillared gateway, which opened upon an avenue of glorious elms. They left the automobile by the roadside with a carelessness of which Guy had not ceased to be conscious, and which never ceased to give him pleasure. To have all the good things, and to have them without the need to guard them, seemed always a holiday of the soul to his twentieth-century mentality, broken to a perpetual defensiveness.

They sauntered up the avenue, enjoying the change of motion. The grounds were more lovely than any Guy had yet seen. He was reminded of the beautiful park of the local magnate in his boyhood—the scene of rare school picnics—but there was a more profuse charm in this modern pleasure-ground. Green vistas

opened up more mysteriously inviting; flowers blazed in glowing masses; there were avenues of great fern-like plants which he
guessed to be palms; fountains splashed; little lakes were revealed
in unsuspected hollows.

"Flowers bloom all the year here," John told him.

"What nonsense are you talking?"

"It is quite true. They have a system of underground heating."

They came to the great marble flight of steps, at the top of
which was a pillared portico. There was an inscription in gold
lettering along the frieze, but as it was in some strange character,
Guy could not read it; and John refused to interpret.

A pleasant-looking young man in a stained blue blouse and
breeches appeared and asked for their permits.

John laughed. "No, we haven't come for that," he said. "Not
yet. My friend here is a stranger and wants to look round. Is there
anyone inside now?"

The young man shook his head. "They come much more often
in the evening," he said. "That's curious, now, isn't it?"

"I perceive that you are an intellectual, but not a psychologist,"
John said, smiling. "Why are you doing this work?"

"I am a botanist." The young man laughed frankly at the hit.
"Out of my work hours I am free to experiment in the grounds."

"I see. May we go round alone?"

The doorkeeper nodded, and they stepped forward through
folding doors into a covered court where a fountain was playing
among palm trees. As the doors silently closed behind them there
fell a sudden hush; the very drops seemed to soften their splash
on the water in the wide stone basin. They saw glimpses of cool
vistas, pillars, arches, and greenery, but nowhere a sign of humanity. There was noticeable a faint sweet-scentedness in the air. The

sense of stepping into another world, another plane of existence, was so strong that they stood still for a moment, gazing.

The adventure took on for Guy a dream-like quality. He followed his companion, incurious, drowsily content, through the long arcades of a kind of palace city; through courts where fountains always played; past nooks and groves where low tables stood beside cushioned couches, as if for a Roman feast; through indoor gardens with flowers of more gorgeous bloom than any he had ever seen. Nowhere was an opening on to the outside world, and yet everywhere was a gentle, pervading glow, as if of veiled sunlight coming from some invisible source. Guy felt as if he were living in a fairy-tale, as if the child's old forgotten longing for the reality of the fairy-tale were at last being satisfied, the child's secret defiant assertion to the ugly world around it, "I know there can be places like that," were justified at last.

He roused himself once to remark to John on the beauty of the place.

"It was designed by an Eastern architect," John told him. "No one understands art of this kind better than they."

Guy thought that there was a drowsy quality even in John's crisp voice.

They came at last into a great central hall. Around its walls were alcoves, in each of which was a cushioned divan. The murmur of a fountain in the centre was the only sound, until John, stepping forward, pressed a knob in a pillar. Immediately there began a queer, sweet, haunting melody, faint at first like the echo of distant fluting, then swelling until it filled the great place with slow waves of sound.

"What is it?" Guy asked in a hushed voice. Tears had come to his eyes. An exquisite languor passed through his limbs.

"The Song of the Lotus," said John quietly.

"I think," Guy's eyes were half closing, "I will lie on one of these couches for a time and listen… The air has made me sleepy… No reason to hurry, is there?"

Then John laughed. It was the faintest echo of his usual clear peal, but it shattered the atmosphere of the place like a gunshot. Guy shook himself and started.

"Come, it is time we were getting out of this," John muttered.

He gripped Guy's arm and drew him firmly out of the great hall into a courtyard, the strains of the wonderful song following them. He would not pause there, but hurried Guy along a short passage in the direction of the entrance and right to the big doors. As the doors swung open and they came through, Guy gasped at the fresh air, as if he had been struck in the face with a dripping sponge.

The young doorkeeper, who was sitting outside, bending over a book, looked at them with a smile.

"I was about to come looking for you," he said.

"It would soon have been necessary," John said ruefully. "I thought I was too tough for anything of this kind; but when my friend here suggested that we should stop in the Euthanasia hall, I was half inclined to agree with him."

"The strongest strength of mind can't fight chemicals," said the other, raising his eyebrows comically.

They laughed together, while Guy drew in great gulps of the sweet summer air, and the haze of slumber cleared from his brain.

"What was that stuff?" he demanded, as they set off back through the park.

"Amaranthol," John told him. "A new compound since your day, I believe. Harmless, but pleasant in small quantities. The water of the fountains gives it off."

"I see. And now, what on earth is it all for?"

John glanced at him. "You didn't understand what I said to the doorkeeper? It is a Euthanasia centre. 'Euthanasia' means 'Happy Death.'"

"You can't mean—?" Guy stopped short on the road and stared at him.

"It is a new idea to you?... Yet even in your days there were men humane enough to protest against prolonging the lives of people who were hopelessly diseased or insane or unsocial."

Guy clutched desperately at the new conception. "I see. Such people are allowed to come here and to end their lives easily if they wish?"

"In some instances," John said, smiling a little, "the wish is not theirs. These establishments were for them originally. Then there are suicides, too... I see that startles you. People were still apt to regard suicide as a crime in your day, weren't they? We are not so foolish as that now; I believe there are still old laws against it in existence, but they are never applied. It's so obvious that, if a man wants to die, he is probably better dead... I suppose he was considered to be robbing his master of valuable property in feudal and competitive times... The State does not openly encourage it, you understand, but, if one really wants a permit, it is not very difficult to get it."

Guy's mind was flying here and there like a bewildered bird. "And if we had stayed in that hall—?" he said.

"As soon as anyone lies on one of the divans a stronger local current is automatically turned on," said John. Guy shivered. "It is a delightful death, as you can judge for yourself."

"And do many people—?" Again the question broke off short; but John answered it.

"Oh yes, a considerable number—chiefly normals in an emotional *impasse*. It is they who like this kind of setting. Intellectuals find life too interesting as a rule, though there are always melancholic types who are apt to turn this way. But there are no Chattertons pulled down by circumstances now. I know there was a legend in your times that artists were a morbid, unstable type; but that was because the conditions of life nearly always involved them in an acute mental conflict between their creative impulse and their social obligations, such as would have driven a normal man completely insane. In our age the artists are the staid, respectable class who marry, and refrain from suicide."

The words fell meaningless on Guy's ears. His head swam. It was as if a pit of darkness had opened under his feet which he must either leap over or pitch into headlong. In its refusal to accept the position, his mind caught momentarily at a support it would commonly have disdained.

"You said many people were religious now. How do they reconcile that with this?"

"They don't entirely," John laughed. "The Church fought it a hundred years ago on the issue of incurable disease and lunacy. No member of theirs was allowed to use it. But both the medicals and the economists became so strongly in favour of this method of dealing with lunacy that in the end there was legislation to enforce it. For some time now the Church has maintained a dignified silence on the subject, just as it has on that of informal unions. But individual preachers here and there still have their tilt at both."

"You can't have many lunatics now?"

For once John hesitated slightly, and Guy was conscious of a certain discomfort in his answer when it came. "We still have them," he said, "even though they are never allowed to breed, neither they nor the feeble-minded, who used to stock half England. It is the one disease that has not been practically conquered. Fits of lunacy are fairly common among normals; they shade off into *crimes passionnelles*, of course." The crimson headline of the newspaper sheet flashed across Guy's recollection.

John was going on. "There are inevitably a great many of those crimes, for the reason that I explained to you this morning. So much more attention is concentrated on the emotions now than used to be when all one's energy was spent in getting a living. It is a necessary by-product of progress. Everyone understands that. People are generally let off for a first offence nowadays, just as a dog is allowed its first bite. But if there is a second, then society has to be protected against them, and they are classed with the lunatics. That is to say, they come here."

"You punish murderers by bringing them here!"

"We don't punish them at all," said John with quick disdain. "Vindictive justice is one of the things which made itself so obnoxious, it could not be endured any longer. The idea is disgusting to any modern mind—hardly better than plain lynching or public flogging. What we do is to try to prevent crime. Emotional violence is almost the only crime we have to deal with, since the property troubles that used to clog your courts have vanished. If people show themselves habitually violent, they have to be removed from society."

Guy was about to ask how large was the number of such crimes, but a misgiving stopped him. The conversation had disturbed him profoundly. For the first time, he found himself utterly unable to accept a reality of the new age. A fantastic horror played about the whole experience, intensified because he had set out to explore the lovely place so lightheartedly, thinking it devoted to some pleasant purpose. John had let him do so, and yet John was obviously unconscious of any brutality. This indifference and the young doorkeeper's careless chat, even the fact that Guy had liked him, seemed in retrospect like some evil practical joke, now that he had to associate the thing with Death. To him, Death was irretrievably associated with fear and shame and pain, with black mourning garments and an awful solemnity. To make it a matter of choice, to surround it deliberately with luxury and charm, struck him like a blasphemy. And there seemed to be something in his inward repulsion that had root even deeper than this.

An instinctive certainty that he would not be understood prevented him from revealing his misgivings to John, and this sense of having lost his guide increased his distress. The chasm of psychological difference gaped at last hopelessly between them— the gap of nearly two centuries of thought and development. He was panic-stricken lest John should perceive it also. So long as he did not, it would not seem so irreparable; it might be possible to ignore it. The terror of isolation was on him again. In his search for concealment, he seized hastily on a point in John's last speech and began to discuss feverishly, as they passed down the drive, the principle of preventive justice.

VI

They stopped short as they came out of the gate into the road again. On the wide grass border just opposite, where had been green empty space an hour ago, was a dense little knot of people clustered about a speaker who was raised head and shoulders above them. He was facing in their direction and pointing at the great gate, so that they themselves, issuing from it, seemed to fall for a moment under the ban of his outstretched arm. They could not yet distinguish the features of the speaker, but Guy saw that the upper part of his body, visible above the heads of the group, was covered by a rough brown stuff, and that, in strange contrast, the hair around the tonsure gleamed with a golden tint in the sunshine.

"Ah!" John gave an interested grunt. "There we have it. A friar preaching against the gilded iniquity. Shall we step across and listen for a moment? He looks an interesting type."

They crossed the road and joined the stragglers at the edge of the group, which was being increased by passers-by at every moment. Guy heard low exclamations of "Father Emmanuel!" passing round, as if the name were a familiar one. He looked curiously at the speaker. He was a man hardly past his youth, approaching middle-age, soft lines of experience about the mouth contradicting the smoothness of his forehead. He had an air of gentleness and refinement. But what gave the face its peculiar quality was the wonderful benevolence of its expression. There was peace in the quiet features and a glow, as of happy love, in the eyes. It was not the face of an ascetic, rather an artist's ideal of the gentle angel, Gabriel.

The preacher's voice was low and penetrating, so that it reached the fringes of the little crowd without any suggestion of strain. It was not, as they had expected, denunciatory, but appealing.

Guy listened for some moments without understanding.

"There was the test of blood and the test of hunger and the test of toil; and now is the day of the test of pleasure. Children, have you not all that you desire?—delicious foods, fine clothing, riches; and if you still must die, you may die here with music and feasting and pleasure-bearing vapours. Children, are you not happy?"

The tone changed; a passionate vibration came into the voice.

"My dear ones, I will not mock you. I know that you have no happiness in these things. Too well I know it, for I have suffered even as you. The craving of the heart cannot be satisfied by these blisses of the body. Are you beasts that perish that you should be content with such as these? As the hart pants for the watersprings, so are you panting, suffering, yes, dying, for the eternal love of Christ, man's only true love.

"God has sent you all the good things of the world in these latter days, that you might know their insufficiency and turn to Him. Will you not understand? Why do you seek to escape from Him who looks for you in tenderness and sorrow? But you run hither and thither, and the fire in your hearts will not let you rest. It drives you, so that you do strange things in your madness and hurt and kill one another, and come hither seeking death because you can bear your agony no longer. But I say to you that even after death, and through all worlds, His love will still pursue you. And only when it finds you at last will you also find peace."

Guy heard John murmur under his breath, "Homœopathic remedy!" and felt a quick impulse of anger against him. Many of the crowd were openly weeping, and he was himself moved. The preacher's mere presence, apart from his words, had that curious effect, inherent in some personalities, of altering accepted proportions, almost of transmuting the plane of experience, so that it was impossible from the first moment to think of him as measured by ordinary standards, or to compare him with other men. And he roused, too, a longing to get into relationship with him, that suggestion of a waiting love and understanding, innocent of all touch of scorn, to obtain which human beings, so brutal and contemptuous towards each other, will go to any pain or sacrifice. The voice sounded again, more strongly.

"Do you not understand that you are Christ's chosen, you in whom burns the flame of love? To you He comes, to the afflicted and distressed, to the humble and the bewildered, to children and to the simple. But to those who rejoice in the pride of their intellects and say to themselves, 'We are as gods,' He will say, 'I never knew you.'"

John laughed quietly and murmured, "*Touché*," adding, "Some of these religious are wonderfully telepathic."

But the preacher was not looking at them. He was speaking into the heart of the crowd, with an intimate, appealing gesture of outstretched hands.

"It is not to them, but to you, I speak. My children, I know how you have suffered, for the discipline of love is a terrible thing. But all this draws to its end. God's angel spoke to me by night—" There was a movement and a murmur of awe in the crowd, but no expression of surprise or incredulity. Guy felt John's figure at his side stiffen with attention.

"He said: 'Go, tell my children that their cry has come to Me, and the prayers of my beloved, crying, "How long?" The days of the earth are wellnigh accomplished; soon shall the Christ be revealed, coming in glory to claim His own. Then shall all that is crooked be made straight, all that are hungry shall be satisfied, and all that are weary shall be at rest. Every man shall be reconciled with his brother, and the love of God shall encompass all.'

"And again he said: 'Bid my children prepare to meet my Son. Let them think no more of food or drink, of fine garments and soft couches; and let there be no more marrying and giving in marriage, for the day of these things is past. Behold, He comes quickly.'"

The preacher stopped and covered his face with his hands for a moment, as if overcome with emotion.

"Have you had enough?" John's voice said in Guy's ear.

Guy roused himself out of his stupefaction. He glanced round as he turned to follow. The intense absorption of the crowd troubled him. A girl in the front rank had knelt silently beside the low stool on which the friar was standing, and remained there quite still, with the border of his robe pressed against her forehead. He had glanced down at her momentarily with an infinite compassion, not pausing in his speech.

Guy suffered a sense of dislocation in walking away from the group, so potent had been its spiritual atmosphere.

As they moved away John made a curious sound, expressive of a surprised, reflective interest, and went on to a queerly irrelevant question.

"Have you seen any reproductions of Paul Martel's Cartoons of the Hallucinated?"

Guy, staring, said that he had not.

"He was an odd combination of scientist and artist," John explained. "He visited one of the old asylums before they were done away with and painted portraits of many of the inmates. Underneath he wrote the delusions from which the subject suffered. The result was extraordinary—the melancholics were like sculptors' personifications of despair. Those who had definite delusions of personality reproduced the people they imagined themselves to be better than the most brilliant actor could do it. There is one young girl who thought herself the Virgin Mary; she was painted nursing a doll, and the painting is always quoted as the most perfect expression of maternal devotion that has ever been produced."

They had reached the car, and he was standing still beside it, absorbed in the interest of his subject.

"But why do you mention it now?" Guy asked in bewilderment.

"Only because that man's face interests me. Its benevolence is divine... I think we shall hear of him again..."

Something passed between them and the sun, and he stopped to glance up.

A small aeroplane was settling on the grass close by them. From it there stepped three men, two of them in dark blue uniform which still distinguished the police. The third, a short slim figure, shrunken together, with drooping head, they helped out, and, taking each an arm, began to move with him towards the gates, glancing curiously round at the crowd as they did so. The preacher had broken off abruptly as the aeroplane landed, and his hearers had turned in sympathy, following his gaze. With a curious motion like melting snow, those who stood between him and the little group seemed to pass into their neighbours, so that in a few seconds a passage opened between them. For a moment there was a total silence. Then, as if in response to that penetrating look, the young man between the warders threw up his head, glanced wildly round until his eyes met the other's and were held. Crying out something inarticulate, he sprang from between his guards before they could make any movement, and dashed down the avenue opened before him towards the preacher.

John exclaimed and began to run back towards the crowd, slipping past the aeroplane. Guy followed him, his heart beating wildly. He had recognised the young man instantly in the second that he had looked up. They edged their way through where the crowd was thinnest and won to a place within a few yards of the friar. He had stepped down from his little platform, and his arms were about the body of the young man, who was weeping wildly against his shoulder. The two warders had followed him part way and stood there, awkwardly hesitating. The crowd kept an absolute stillness and silence; it seemed to be all eyes.

The young man's voice came hysterical and abandoned through the hush. "Oh, Father, I don't want to die. I can't die... Save me! save me!" He was making motions as if to kneel, but Emmanuel prevented him.

"Hush, hush, my son, my little child—" The friar's thrilling voice stirred like wind in the dawn. "A little affliction, a little pain, now... There is no death... Yet a little while; submit now to the evils of men... The mercy of God is at hand... You have sinned—do not tell me; I know it all... But you have loved much... Christ has already forgiven you. See, I weep with you... Our sweet human weakness... Yet before the year be out, you and I shall sit together in Paradise."

"Father, must I go... must I... must I?" Brady had drawn himself a little away now, and was standing, a small dishevelled figure, his life concentrated in the appeal of his eyes.

"My beloved, how gladly would I come with you!" The friar put his hands on the young man's shoulders and looked at him lovingly. "But I may not yet. I must remain and do what is appointed me to do... Now you shall share with me the Bread of Heaven, Christ's love-feast. We will eat and drink together, and then you will pass on ahead of us. A little while, such a little while."

The scene that followed had a solemnity and yet a simple homeliness that was almost unbearably poignant. The people knelt around the preacher on the grass and took their sacrament from him—bread and wine from crude earthenware vessels. He talked to them as he administered it, not in the manner of an officiating priest, but friend to friend, as Jesus Himself might have talked to His disciples. Guy could not hear all that was said; with one or two others, he and John had drawn back from the circle. As they watched from the background, a sense of shameful intrusiveness came over him, yet he could not remove his eyes from Emmanuel and the small figure crouching at his feet.

The two warders had exchanged a few words, and then apparently decided not to interfere. They waited, standing isolated in the road between the kneeling group around the friar and the palace gates. Emmanuel, looking up, beckoned to them to come. They wavered; one of them took a few steps forward, stopped, then strode swiftly to join the kneelers. His companion looked after him a moment and then turned his back.

When everyone who would had received the sacrament, the friar went back to George Brady and raised him to his feet. With an arm round his shoulders, still talking to him quietly, he began to walk with him towards the Euthanasia Palace gate. They passed near to Guy, and he saw that Brady's eyes were gazing straight before him, glazed as if he had been hypnotised. The crowd, following slowly at a little distance, came between and prevented him from seeing the moment of parting at the gates; but as he came up he saw that one of the warders, the one who had turned his back, had lingered behind the two figures that were passing alone up the avenue. His hand was on the friar's sleeve.

"Father, forgive… forgive… I did not…"

Emmanuel looked at him compassionately. "To you also it shall be forgiven, my son," he said, "and to all that know not what they do. Go in peace!"

The warder muttered something and hurried after the others.

Emmanuel turned his wonderful eyes, bright with tears, upon the waiting people. "Forgive me, my children," he said, "and leave me now a little. I must weep for our brother awhile and pray for him in his passing. Presently return to me and I will talk with you again. But now, go."

A sigh so profound that it was almost a sob went up from the crowd. They began obediently to disperse. The friar pulled forward his cowl until it almost concealed his face and walked away, his head bent towards the ground.

VII

They went to their car and climbed in silently.

"I wish Alexis had seen this," John murmured as he started the engine.

They were silent for a time. Then Guy burst out abruptly, startling himself:

"*He* didn't want to die, in spite of all your Euthanasia."

John raised his eyebrows. "I suppose the anticipation is always dreadful to full-blooded people. The most that can be done is to make the process itself as easy as possible. Do you think your method of hanging was to be preferred?"

Guy paused, swallowing. "Yes," he said violently. "Yes. It was not so horrible—not so damnably hypocritical."

John smiled. "It affects you in that way?" he said thoughtfully. "None the less, I believe that if you had to choose, you would prefer to die in the modern manner. Come now, wouldn't you? You should be a judge of modes of dying."

Guy turned pale. An impulse to ignore the last suggestive sentence at any cost almost carried him away; then, in a quick reaction, fully aware that he was challenging some great peril, he demanded hoarsely, "What do you mean by that?"

John glanced at him, and his face became concerned. "I am sorry. I ought not to have said it. I ought to have remembered that it might still be a sensitive point... I had better go on now. You haven't yet realised that you were the first success in my uncle's attempt to reintegrate and revive dead bodies? I hope you will not be the only one; but it begins to appear as if it might be so. They gave him an old burying-ground where the soil is preservative; and the conditions, apart from that, seem to have been unusually favourable in your case. Perhaps you will be able to explain that to us some day?"

Guy began to shiver as if he had a sudden attack of fever. The sweat poured from his body. His mind gasped and floundered, conscious only of struggling in a black, overwhelming sea.

John pulled up at an inn and got him some brandy. He was disturbed and remorseful and called himself a fool. Guy realised these external incidents, as he agonised to win some control over the monstrous impressions that strove and mounted in his brain, to save his identity from the seething chaos. It was as if some dam had broken and let loose the flood upon him. And, meanwhile, the external, observing portion of his mind understood and was even piqued by the fact that John, in all his remorse, thought his intense agitation curious and, in some way, slightly despicable.

"You must go to my uncle as soon as you reach home," he told him, "and ask him to make fresh suggestions to you. The first ones have evidently become weakened, and you are not yet able to do without… You know, of course, that he hypnotised you to break the shock of your awakening?"

Guy nodded. All the things which he had accepted without thought, with what he now realised to have been an artificially induced disregard, were rushing through his consciousness, blazing in full significance, like comets in the darkness. His pleasant life of the last few weeks had become a flimsy veil thrown over reality, and now flying loose in shreds. It was not he himself, in the completeness of his personality, who had lived them. Now he was struggling, violently and assertively, to be himself again. He clung to that, even while he still shrank from the enormity of the experiences through which he knew that his soul and body had come.

He felt afresh the impulse to hide himself from John. It seemed vital that no one should know what was taking place within him. He began to talk again as naturally as he could, while they ran swiftly back into the town; and the mere effort helped him towards mental collectedness. John was evidently reassured, for he put him down at the gates of the Wayland grounds, and, with only a fresh word of advice to consult Dr. Wayland at once, hurried on to keep an engagement for which he was already late.

Guy stood still until he was out of sight. Then, with a final half-longing, half-hostile glance at where the white walls of the house gleamed among the trees, turned sharply away and began to walk towards an inn which he knew, some distance down the river.

CHAPTER IX

EMMANUEL

I

GUY'S NERVOUS CRISIS LASTED WITH VARYING INTENSITY for several days, but always moving towards recovery. He did not at bottom realise even now the monstrosity of his renewed existence, but only the fact that it was monstrous. He forced himself to the conception of his tranced body lying through years and decades in its coffin, stirring, then half alive, under Dr. Wayland's inconceivable processes; but he could not vitally connect it with his existing conscious self, any more than a man can think of himself as a babe issuing from his mother's womb. "Twice-born," the favourite Theosophist phrase, came back to him: it was true in a practical sense in his own case.

Yet the only realities seemed to be his present physical self and the continuity of his mental experience.

The weeks that he had passed under the influence of Dr. Wayland's suggestions had, in fact, broken the worst of the shock for him, as it had been intended that they should. He was in relation with his environment; he knew what to do and what to say. He was able to live at the inn as an ordinary traveller, and found it tranquillising to be among people who did not know that there was anything exceptional about him. Nevertheless they were bad days. He did not sleep at night, and spent the daytime wandering about the country, keeping most often to the open heaths south of the river. They were days pervaded by an almost intolerable loneliness. The passions and preoccupations of the old times had not come back with his recovery of an individual outlook; they still seemed distant and colourless; his recent life remained the more vivid. And yet in regard to that, every perspective was altered. All conclusions had to be revised; all relationships reconsidered. He felt himself face to face, quite alone now, with an alien world, and without the strength or wit to cope with it.

No aid, human or divine, reached him through these days of desolation. It was something more elementary, a sub-human contact, uncursed by self-consciousness, that brought him the humble kind of comfort that alone could have reached him, and which perhaps saved him from crossing the borderline of sanity. A mongrel terrier unaccountably attached himself to him, and would follow him on his lonely expeditions. This creature was accustomed to haunt the inn, though he belonged, they said, to a neighbouring "animal woman"—one of a type occurring occasionally in the old times, but now apparently become common—a solitary who lived surrounded by animal pets. At the inn the dog was alternately brutally teased or sickeningly petted, no one there appearing to have any understanding of dog nature. Guy thought, shrugging, that it must be his own complete disregard that had attracted the creature, and yet Ben's devotion warmed his heart a little. One day when he had suffered a complete breakdown and lay weeping in a hidden hollow, Ben threw himself upon him in such distress, whining and licking his face and hands, that he was compelled to laugh. For a moment he reeled on the verge of hysteria, then recovered his composure with a wrench. He sat for a long time talking childishly to the dog with his arm about his neck, comforted by the living warmth of his body, telling him all the things which it was impossible that he should say to any human being.

This proved to be the turning-point. Guy found his curiosity reviving. He began to talk to his neighbours. The same evening he telephoned to John.

II

Guy had taken the precaution (a sign of fundamental poise which might have reassured him, if he had been a psychologist) of telephoning to the Waylands the evening of his flight, saying that he intended to travel about the country and would not be coming back for a short time. He knew that in this highly civilised society such an announcement would be received as simply as a proposal to go for a walk. Dr. Wayland—he recognised it now with a rueful smile—would probably not notice his absence at all. He rang off in the middle of one of Agatha's monologues without giving any clue to his whereabouts.

John appeared after his second message, nonchalant as ever, saying very little about Guy's movements, beyond the remark:

"So you did not go to my uncle after all?"

The tone was casual, but its very casualness had a further implication. Guy understood from it that John was speaking to him again as to an equal; that infinitesimal suggestion of disdain, which only a hypersensitive listener would have detected, had vanished. John's uncompromising realism was satisfied by his refusal to go back to the deceptive mental ease offered by hypnotic suggestion.

It was like John's own refusal to be affected by the amaranthol in the Euthanasia Palace.

Outwardly they took up their friendship where they had left it. But Guy recognised with a pang of regret that their relations had changed and would remain different. His own new mental attitude made that inevitable. He could no longer go out to John in a childlike expansiveness, but watched him cautiously, arming himself with secretiveness, eager, but distrustful.

Whether John recognised the difference or not he had no means of knowing, though his knowledge of John's ruthlessly keen intelligence made it seem probable that he did. However, he gave no sign of it, but talked gaily as ever on every topic that offered itself, took Guy for expeditions, gave him all the practical help and hints that he needed. Only when Guy, sickened by his mental solitude, occasionally approached in gusts of impulse the verge of more intimate confidences, was there an indefinable withdrawal, and he knew that John was telling him inexorably:

"You have chosen to face facts for yourself. Very well, face them out. I respect your attitude, and I shall not spoil it by helping you… Anything else I can do…"

At times this unuttered exhortation braced Guy; at times he rebelled against its austerity. This harsh country of intellectual independence came so easily to John, grown up in its clear, cold atmosphere; so painfully to his own confused, composite, twentieth-century nature, weakened by mental opiates and old indulgences.

Beyond casual allusions, John said nothing of the Wayland family all this time. And Guy, though he sometimes wondered, did not question him.

III

There was at the inn a little grey-haired elderly man called Howard. He was one of the few permanent residents, not because he needed the "vagabond's wage," being in receipt of all his coupons, but because he had himself been the inn manager throughout his work period. His wife had died there, and he had never had the heart to leave the place, after his official position had passed from him. There had been three managers since that time, but Howard stayed on, and was taken for granted now, as if he had been a piece of the furniture.

He spent the greater part of his time in his rooms on the top floor. Guy was told that he kept them under lock and key and would allow no one but himself to go in. When he was downstairs among his fellow-guests, he seemed bent on self-effacement. His little bright eyes gleamed in watchful defensiveness, like those of some small animal; he slipped in and out with sidelong furtiveness, and never spoke unless the necessity was forced upon him.

Guy was amazed when, one day, he made an advance to him. It was part of a larger astonishment which he had felt from the beginning of his stay at the inn—that, even while his first morose mood lasted, and more later on, people had attached themselves to him. They were attracted, apparently, like Ben the dog, by nothing but his quietness and reticence. Among themselves, they seemed to have little intercourse other than feuds, bickerings, and dislike. He found himself the recipient of confidences from all sides; his society competed for. The gourmet addressed to him his criticisms of the dishes. A middle-aged and spreading woman with dyed hair would pour out to him the stories of her past love affairs. She liked to hold Ben while she did so, handling him as if he also were a lover, while the dog's patient eyes would wander appealingly to Guy from under the load of hugs and kisses. The only persons who did not fasten upon Guy in this manner had been Howard and a travelling intellectual, who stayed one night in the house, but passed on the next morning.

Guy wavered between a certain gratification, for he had never experienced popularity before, and an increasing boredom which sometimes reached a positive nervous shrinking from his neighbours. Of genuine intercourse they afforded him nothing; in all their conversations he realised that he was not expected, nor desired, to speak, beyond an occasional sympathetic murmur; and inwardly he found himself constrained by them into the adult attitude towards children, just as it had been with Ena.

At times he had hoped that John would suggest his removal to the Bachelor Chambers. But John never did, and Guy realised that this was of a piece with John's somewhat terrible respect for his independence. A certain pride prevented him from making the change on his own initiative.

Then one day the old man, Howard (he was not much over sixty, but he gave the effect of age), touched him on the arm on the stairs, glancing this way and that to make sure that there were no listeners.

"Come. I've—I've got something to show you." His voice gasped and trembled, and Guy saw that his whole body was shaking.

He followed him, wondering. The little man led him quickly up to his rooms at the top of the house, stopping to peer round every corner. As they came to his door, he gave a quick glance at Guy, oddly compounded of eagerness and distrust. Then, as if afraid that he might never do it if he hesitated, pulled his key hurriedly from his waistband and thrust it into the lock. The door swung open.

"I'm to come in?" Guy said doubtfully.

"Come, come." The other pulled at him with a frantic gesture, slammed the door behind him, and locked it as if he were just in time to shut out a pursuing enemy.

"Now look," he said.

Around the room, which was otherwise bare, were an array of glass cases set out on tables. Guy shivered. The old man's sudden confidence after his habitual secretiveness, his queerness and furtive behaviour, suggested to him some horror. His nerves were not yet perfectly recovered.

To settle the matter, he stepped quickly over to one of the cases, and immediately had a convulsive struggle to suppress the laugh which rose to his throat. This marvel, behind locked doors, guarded so closely, watched over so jealously, was a collection of buttons!

They lay there, buttons of all sorts and sizes, ancient and modern, metal, stone, wood, bone, linen buttons; buttons carved and smooth, round and angular. Each rested in a separate velvet setting.

Guy stood still for a moment with his back to Howard. He realised that at all costs he must not show his feelings. Whatever else it was, this preposterous collection was obviously the mainspring of the old man's life.

"This is a wonderful collection," he said at last, turning back to him.

The expression of agonised anxiety on the wrinkled little face gave place to one of relief. Guy saw, with impotent pity, what this endorsement of his life's passion meant to the little man. If he had shown contempt it would have been almost enough to kill him, or to drive him completely crazy.

Howard sprang forward to his side with a grasshopper-like movement, and began to talk with the precipitancy of the silent man released at last from his inhibition. He poured it all out, the words falling over one another—stories of how he had got the collection together, where he had found this and that treasure, how he had ransacked the sites of old houses, how he spent half his coupons in buying clothes he did not need in order to keep his collection up to date, what pains he had gone to that its existence might be kept secret from all the world.

"Not that there are many people who would know how to value a collection like this," he said; "but there are always one or two who know. They'd do anything to get some of these specimens. Don't you think so?" Again came that eager, suspicious look, avid for confirmation.

"No doubt," Guy assented, his heart aching.

The old man wandered on. "You know I'm descended from the Norfolk Howards. I suppose it's in the blood. They knew how to gather fine things around them, those old aristocrats. It wasn't like this age, when everyone lives just the same."

Guy identified a twentieth-century army button, to Howard's quivering delight. "I knew you were a connoisseur. I recognised it at once. I saw immediately that if I could ever show my collection to anyone it would be you. You must forgive me that I was so long in coming to a decision. But it is necessary to be very careful, as you see."

After this, Guy found it impossible to upset the legend of his connoisseurship. Howard was constantly bringing him to see some new specimen, always with the same precautions.

He would nod and wink at him across the table at mealtimes with joyous secretiveness. But when they talked together Guy noticed that he always turned the conversation so as to elicit some expression of admiration for the collection from Guy himself. Having got this, he would take a breath of relief, and chatter on cheerfully again.

IV

But personal preoccupations at this time were subjected to an invasion of a kind with which Guy had been familiar in his early days, which had been days of events and of public uneasiness, days of great strikes, of wars, of massacres and revolutions. These things would begin with a vague paragraph in the news-papers, like a cloud no bigger than a man's hand; they would heap up, loom larger, and at last overspread the sky, obscuring for the time all individual interests with the dark drama of their development.

Such an interruption now occurred even in the placid, well-ordered public life of the twenty-second century.

It began for Guy now also in a newspaper paragraph which John laughingly showed to him, inserted in the single remaining page which was still innocent of lurid description of crimes of violence, and was devoted to such political news as remained, to public announcements and events of milder interest. It was a semi-humorous allusion to the doings of a New Franciscan friar, Emmanuel, who was said to be leading an increasing train of people about the outskirts of London, preaching fasting, celibacy, and the imminent approach of the Second Advent.

"I thought we should hear from him again," John said. "He believes what he says, and a man who does that always makes an effect of some sort."

Guy found that he could not take the news so lightly. The preaching of the friar and the little scene at the gates of the Euthanasia Palace were indissolubly associated for him with the shock and revolution in his own mind which had occurred at the same time. He could not escape from a vague but strong impression that there was some peculiar significance in this fresh impinging of the friar upon his experience. But he did his best to conceal this presentiment from John.

He read eagerly every day the lengthening account of Father Emmanuel's doings—how his following increased hourly; how men knelt to him in public, weeping and confessing their sins; how he slept on the ground and ate almost nothing; how a factory by which he passed had been brought to a standstill by the desertion of its workers. Soon the reports began to invade even the pages devoted to crimes and horrors.

Sometimes there would be recorded an incident headed: "A new St. Francis," or some such title. It was told how Emmanuel had kept waiting a deputation from the London bishops while he visited a bedridden old woman who could not come to him, and again how he had talked all one night to a Buddhist monk, who had gone away persuaded that he was a reincarnation of Gautama. But there were also stories of a different character. One priest who had attempted to call away members of his congregation from Emmanuel's following had been terribly questioned, with questions unintelligible to the bystanders, but obviously of fearful significance to the man himself, who had ended by falling in a faint. He had been taken back to his house, and there Emmanuel had visited him alone the next day. He was now one of the most devoted of the friar's disciples.

At last one day came the news of a miracle—how Emmanuel's shadow in passing had fallen upon and cured a paralysed child.

"I inquired afterwards," the report stated, "and ascertained with certainty that this was a genuine case of paralysis from the earliest months of life. Doctors had been unable to do anything for it. True, it was paralysis, the class of case always known to be most amenable to psychological suggestion. But one is apt to forget all that when one actually sees the pale face, the recumbent form, and crippled limbs, and then, five minutes later, sees the same child running and laughing joyfully, embraced and wept over by his parents, while the author of their happiness passes quietly on in his gentle, radiant beneficence. This remarkable incident must swell the prestige of Father Emmanuel. Many who were inclined to scoff at his tremendous claims and startling prophecies are beginning to ask themselves, with the quick-drawn breath of wonder, 'What if, after all, there should be something in it?'"

On this dramatic question the report stopped short.

"These sham intellectuals!" John chuckled over the journalist's effort. "They are always so incurably atmospheric. Never, never, never do they say what they mean. I believe they don't even know."

v

As Emmanuel's career began to throw its fierce colouring over the quiet shades of everyday life, Guy became too much absorbed in it to notice that he was no longer invited to the top room where

Howard kept his astonishing collection. He was restlessly interested in all that concerned the friar. He could not shake off the notion that here, in some form, was the key to all his perplexities. He read all the newspapers on which he could lay hands, and questioned everyone who came with news of the movement. Yet when he heard that Emmanuel was passing quite near and would probably preach at a bridge a little distance down the river, he found himself unwilling to go. Now that it came to the point of action, his reason and his old agnostic bias proved too strong for the new fancy. He could not go as in search of enlightenment; nor yet could he go, as John might, for amusement. In the end, he stayed in the house that day.

It was a surprise to him to learn, as he talked to the young present manager of the inn, that Howard had been one of those who had set out to hear the preacher.

"He's been taking a great interest in all these doings just lately," the man said. "Haven't you noticed? He seems to have taken to you. I never saw him do that with anyone before. But they all have." He sighed a little. "When I finish my term next year," he added without apparent connection, "I am going to help a friend of mine to search for rare gulls. He's an intellectual," he added with a touch of defiance, "but we get on well together."

Guy murmured some response. It pleased him to hear that the old man had gone to Emmanuel with the rest, but it astonished him as well. He had not supposed any such diversion from his monomania possible to him. It seemed almost like a hint of remaining mental balance in Howard—this same action which Guy had denied to himself as superstitious folly.

He watched anxiously for the old man's return; but he did not come back that night.

The next morning he appeared, but slipped upstairs quietly before anyone could speak to him. Later, in the after-lunch quiet, Guy saw him slip out again by the side door. He was carrying a large leather bag. Guy hesitated; then that absurd, inexplicable faint sense of responsibility which all these people aroused in him, combined with a certain pitying affection which he had developed unawares for the old man since his grotesque confidences, perhaps also a touch of curiosity, overcame his reluctance to be involved in further extravagances. He followed.

As he came up beside him, Howard started and turned pale.

"You aren't going away from us, surely?" Guy asked in a hearty tone.

The old man did not answer.

"Come. Tell me what you have got in that bag."

Howard turned on him suddenly eyes glittering with excitement.

"I am going to burn them," he said fiercely.

"What? Not—?"

"Yes, all of them." Howard nodded vehemently.

"But—! Your splendid collection! Surely you won't—?" Guy stopped short, at a loss. He could not guess at the other's mental state.

"They were splendid, weren't they?" Howard darted at him one of his old side-glances. "You were the only one who understood that." He lingered a moment, then took a breath and passed on. "But she wouldn't understand. She would think I was wasting my life collecting buttons... I shouldn't like to show them to her... And when I have her again... I shan't want... A young man, too."

Guy stared at him, convinced that he was raving.

The old man threw him a shrewd glance.

"I'm talking about my wife," he explained in matter-of-fact tones. "He says all this life will soon be finished, and we shall meet them all again, and all be made young and happy. He was so good; you could see he knew... And then I thought what she would say if she knew I'd spent all my life collecting buttons... It—it doesn't seem very manly, does it?... I took to it gradually, you know... I'd found one or two good specimens. I didn't think of it growing as it did. Perhaps I became a little too much absorbed. It is too trivial to occupy a man's whole mind, isn't it?—though very interesting, of course. I've felt that sometimes... He said that God understood everything, and everybody would be forgiven. Only we must leave everything and follow Him so as to be ready for the great day. So I thought I'd finish the collection for good... Anyhow, I don't suppose we shall care much about things of that sort afterwards, do you?"

Guy shook his head.

It was a pathetic little holocaust on the corner of a common. Howard had brought wood and paper. He wept a little before the flames fairly caught, but a happier, steadier look than Guy had ever seen there came over his face as the precious collection blazed up. When it was all consumed, and only bits of shining, fused metal showed among the ashes, he gave a sigh of relief.

"There! I shall be able to face her now... I wonder if she will recognise me. Young again, too." The little man almost strutted. "I must go back to him now. I mean to be among the first... He's so kind, so—beautiful. You feel he understands everything... I told him about the collection and asked what I ought to do; and he said: 'Do what your heart tells you, my son.' Wasn't that wonderful?"

He tried to persuade Guy to go back with him to Emmanuel, ardently anxious that he should share his own blessedness. Guy was touched, for he had never felt before that the other recognised in him any existence except as a receptacle for his own confidences. He refused, but half promised to follow later. As he saw the frail little figure march off, tears gathered in his eyes. It seemed useless to say anything. It was obvious that nothing would disturb Howard's conviction. Could he even be sure that he ought to disturb it? Could, after all, any superstition be worse than a life that centred around buttons?

VI

Then one day came the great startling headlines:

"EMMANUEL CLAIMS TO BE THE MESSIAH.
CAN IT BE TRUE?
END OF THE WORLD PROPHESIED FOR NEXT SUNDAY.
HALF LONDON GOES INTO THE FIELDS."

The paper described scenes of "indescribable" enthusiasm—the flocking of huge multitudes of people out of town and from the surrounding country; there were more miracles and spiritual voices heard; an aura of light had been seen to play about the self-styled Messiah. It was added that the Pope was despatching a special legate to inquire into the new religious movement.

VII

The inn that morning was in a hum of excitement. People came and went restlessly; staff and service were disorganised by the non-arrival of workers from the local Domestic Centre; there was shouting and the excited exchange of news. When Guy came downstairs, breakfastless, he found that there had arrived a man with whom he had shared a bottle of wine two evenings before, a coarsely jovial, loud-laughing man, who had expressed the intention of, "going to look at this preacher fellow." Now, he was back again with a quiet, subdued face and a light of awe in his eyes. He had witnessed the great scene of the previous day, when Emmanuel had proclaimed himself the Christ, had touched his gown, and had been one of the many who had been sent out to tell all who would listen to come to Richmond Hill at dawn on Sunday morning to meet Emmanuel.

His belief was absolute. "I'm not fit to be his messenger," he said in a quivering voice. "I haven't been a good man. He knew that. He said, 'Your life has been without thought, my friend, or remembrance of me. Yet you will love me enough to do this service for me.' I would do anything for him—anything, even if he sends me to hell afterwards."

"But you don't seriously believe—?" Guy could not help breaking in.

"And do you think he would lie to us?" The man turned on him fiercely. "If you'd seen him, you'd know better. I tell you that if this isn't true, there is nothing true in heaven or earth. Men are nothing and God is nothing... But I can't talk to you. If you can't believe me, go and see him for yourself."

Guy did not tell him that he had already seen Emmanuel. And by some psychological twist his view of the effect of that sight on this other man affected him more profoundly than his own experience. Sane or mad, the friar certainly had overwhelming personality. He had brought hundreds of thousands of others to share in his madness. Megalomania on this scale seemed almost beyond human criticism, like a natural cataclysm.

He heard John's voice calling him from the door, and went out to find him bursting with news. It appeared that he had received an emergency call to go and work at a Labourers' Centre owing to the desertion of many of the workers.

"We intellectuals will have to keep things going until this madness is over," he explained. "They'll soon come back after Sunday morning. It's fortunate that he has fixed so early a date for his last day."

His spirits were at schoolboy pitch. There recurred suddenly to Guy a day in the old twentieth-century world when a railway strike was disorganising the country. He remembered how the young assistant-manager at his bank (a post that was practically a sinecure in a certain family) had gone off joyously to take tickets and slam lift-doors on an underground railway along with numbers of other gay young men of the leisured classes who meant to "keep things going until the beggars had had enough of it." The two situations had a startling similarity in difference. He even found a little of his old smarting resentment inexplicably transferring itself to this other debonair young man of the new age. It appeared in a desire to say something aggressive. But it was difficult to find anything; for, after all, what were these young intellectuals doing that was not generally helpful and could harm nobody? In fact, from any sane point of view, they were saving the situation.

Yet the resentment came through. "So your social system is not entirely proof against disorganisation, after all?" he suggested, and there was an edge in his tone.

"No," said John good-humouredly. "Did I ever say it was? These emotional waves among normals throw us out now and then,

though never dangerously. Our arrangements are too nearly automatic. A few trained intellectuals can run the country for a month
or two if necessary. But we have never actually been called upon
before, though we were warned in connection with a spiritualistic
movement a few years ago. One social psychologist said that the
recent communising of food would intensify these things. It may
turn out that he was right."

But he was too much exhilarated to linger theorising. He
exclaimed with delight on hearing that Emmanuel meant to greet
the dawn of the Last Day with his followers on Richmond Hill.

"We'll go!" he exclaimed. "We'll make a party of it. It will
be a fine thing for Alexis—he is just designing a new play with
a religious motif. You'll come too, won't you? It will be a sight
worth seeing."

Guy hesitated. The suggestion, and especially the manner of
it, was intensely distasteful to him, but here, in the face of John's
breezy assumption, he could not find a pretext for refusing it.

He agreed. John, with an air of preternatural importance, went
off to his job at the Labourers' Centre.

VIII

The plain and the lower slopes of the hill were covered with
groups of people. They became visible gradually as the light grew
stronger with approaching dawn; earlier, their presence had been
declared only by a low murmur of whispering voices rising in the
darkness like the surge of the sea. Guy Martin stood on a small
hillock among the little band which had called for him hilariously
before the clock struck midnight.

There were people of all types and nationalities. Guy heard foreign languages spoken close to him, many of which he could not identify. There were black men, yellow men, brown men of every shade. Emmanuel's presence had never been reported outside England; yet his call seemed to have been carried and received beyond the seas. They stretched to the horizon in every direction, these people who had accepted the divinity of a man like themselves; who believed that familiar nature, the sun itself, the green earth, the whole course and swing of the universe throughout space and time, was about to submit itself to the word of one of their own kind; that human emotion, so absolute in its grip on their minds and hearts, was about to prove itself the ultimate conqueror, the sufficient end of all things. They obscured the face of the country with their thousands. Only the crest of the hill itself, a few hundred yards from where Guy was standing, rose bare and empty above the ocean of heads. No one had ventured to set foot on it.

The voices were low, though their aggregate made that surging sound which was like waves beating on a rocky coast. On every face was the same expression of awed anticipation; individuals glanced around them uncertainly and seemed to be comforted in feeling the neighbourhood of their fellows in the tremendous ordeal that was approaching. Guy wondered where Howard was in all this multitude. And yet they seemed to him all to be Howard. They were so childlike, so unable to help themselves, so utterly trustful towards this stupendous promise of help which had reached them from outside.

The barefoot, coarse-robed men who were the more immediate disciples of Emmanuel passed quietly from group to group, confirming and encouraging. Guy saw that on all their faces shone the same steadfast light as he had seen on the face of Emmanuel himself, and that the people looked at them trustfully and timidly, like children who desire to be reassured. There were movements to kiss their hands and the hems of their gowns as they passed. And then the diversion would be over and eyes would turn again to the empty summit of the hill, and round again to the first faint lightening of the sky in the East.

It seemed that so vast an emotion of expectancy must in some way carry its own fulfilment. Yet what exactly did they expect? A pantomime transformation scene like those in the old illustrated Bibles? A mental enlightenment which would alter the whole implication of the sensible world for every living soul? A plunge into a void of spiritual passion like the oblivion of a plunge into a warm bath? Guy did not know, and yet he found himself sharing their expectancy. They trusted Emmanuel, their ideal, the man from whom love radiated, who had known how to touch the inmost core of their souls. There were so many of them… Something must happen.

Sunrise was very near. The Eastern sky was a blend of rose tints bordered by a subtle, exquisite green. And now, suddenly, there was a figure standing on the summit of the hill, his arm outstretched in the act of blessing; and with a sound that was half a sigh, half the moan of satisfied emotion, the great multitude knelt.

IX

Guy became aware that a low conversation was going on near him. A tall dark man, thin and angular, with the intense face of an enthusiast, had approached and was addressing John:

"The Lord is here, and do you stand upright?"

The voice was very quiet, but none the less there was in it the hint of a concealed menace. In a moment Guy became sensible not only of the pathos of the vast waiting multitude, but of its power. He saw that the members of the group from which the speaker had come were following the incident intently. He tingled suddenly with the sense of personal danger.

John studied the face of his antagonist quietly a moment with his clear, disinterested gaze. Then he turned to his companions, who had moved up to listen, a half-smile curving his lips:

"Friends, this joke is against us." He knelt down.

The others, and with them Guy, also knelt, The dark man looked at them uncertainly, hesitated, and moved away.

A hymn was rising from the kneeling people, sung low and quietly, but filling the air with a swelling volume of sound. It rewove for Guy the spell which the little incident had interrupted. He knelt there among the kneeling thousands, even his scoffing companions compelled to submit to the collective impulse, and felt a perfect quiescence. He seemed to be incapable now of further active experience. His mind had been too long exercised and overwhelmed among things too great for it, and now he cared for nothing but to rest, a puppet in the hands of fate. Perhaps the end of it all would come in a few moments.

The first ray of the sun struck up across the horizon and fell upon the face of Emmanuel as he fronted it alone upon the hill. The singing stopped as if it had been cut off with a knife. Emmanuel's face seemed to give out a glory; he gazed into the East, and his hands rose in a rapturous welcome.

He stood thus a moment—two moments. Then, with a loud ringing cry, he pitched forward suddenly and rolled down the slope.

The sun had risen and was shining with its clear, cruel white light upon an unchanged world.

X

For a few seconds there was a dead silence. And then there arose a cry which never afterwards ceased to ring in Guy's ears, a cry, terrible and indescribable, the ultimate disappointment of humanity, the eternal disillusionment, multiplied and intensified a hundred thousand times.

Almost immediately the crowd began to melt away. They slunk off like beaten dogs, each man by himself, crouching, hardly rising from their knees, indifferent to all pride and self-respect. Guy's soul slunk with them, whipped, ashamed, unspeakably defeated.

In aching sorrow and shame he felt it now, the democratic passion, the sense of his oneness with the masses of humanity. And, in the same moment, he knew that he had never felt it before.

As in the distance, he heard John's voice saying:

"I think, Alexis, we may safely get up now."

CHAPTER X

GUY AND JOHN

I

"FAINTED OR DEAD, IT IS THE END OF THIS MESSIAH." THE voices of his party roused Guy from his torpor.

"Poor devil! Someone ought to go and look for him."

"The Red Cross arranged to have a few aeroplanes at hand. They will look after him."

"Who is for breakfast? Religion is hungry work."

"I shall never forget Wayland's pious expression!"

Alexis said thoughtfully:

"This affair has given me ideas. I wonder if they will be back at work to-morrow? I have enjoyed snapping switches at the power station as a change, but I shall want to catch this impression while it is fresh."

John laughed and said:

"Most of them will be back to-morrow—all who are not drunk. Even a normal's religion won't stand up against such a cold shower-bath as this."

Guy's body seemed to act without his volition. He stared at his hand the next moment in dull astonishment, aware that he had suddenly whirled round and struck John a violent blow in the face with his clenched fist.

John staggered back, throwing up his hands to his face. For a moment no one moved or spoke. Then John, recovering, glanced quietly round at the company.

"Martin and I are going to walk home," he said. "I shall see you all again later on."

The others instantly said pleasant good-byes that completely ignored the incident, and set off in ones and twos in their several directions. John, drawing Guy after him with a glance, began to make for the London road.

II

The conversation which followed, and which lasted intermittently for several hours, was feverish, unsatisfactory, incoherent. Its superficial form did not express the reality of it, which was a psychological conflict that Guy did not understand, but knew instinctively to be of essential importance. His quiescence had passed with the blow, and his mind was swayed by emotions that surged like waves driven back upon each other by opposing forces. His hatred of this man at his side was inflamed by lingering idealistic love for him. Throughout the interview his speech evaded his intentions, striking off into irrelevancies in spite of him, in a fashion that exasperated him almost to madness; and he was quite unaware that at times he came nearer to eloquence than ever before in his life.

John, on the other hand, was cool, even kind, for the most part, and nothing he said gave any handle against him, although his manner of speech was, as always, quick and easy.

One of those maddening irrelevancies leapt off Guy's tongue at the very beginning of the conversation, as they walked away from the scattering members of the party which had left them so obviously in obedience to John's prompting.

He said: "You are treating me like a normal who is making a scene."

"Aren't you behaving like one?" John asked gently.

The place on his cheek where Guy's fist had caught him was already beginning to turn purple. It fascinated Guy, so that his eyes kept going back to it. As if he divined this, John took an opportunity, as they turned into the riverside road, to move to the other side of him. Guy hated him anew, with a fervour that astonished himself, for his magnanimity.

"Tell me what it is." John's voice had the ring of authority. And, for that, too, Guy hated him, even while his tongue stumbled to obey him.

"It was because you laughed—your horrible laugh."

John raised his eyebrows.

"How dare you laugh at those people? Who are you to laugh at them?"

"But who could help laughing? One doesn't laugh because one is anybody in particular, but because a thing is laughable… Come, there was no harm done, you know… They will all find new excitements within a day or two. Normals always do."

Guy burst out: "They are not normal. How can you call them that? They are morbid and hysterical, everyone of them. I've seen. It is horrible. They do all sorts of queer things. There isn't one of them that wouldn't have been called a crank in the old times… It was the same before. Ena and Terry and Agatha, all of them, only I wouldn't see it then… Normal!"

John frowned. "You are using words carelessly," he said. "The normal thing is, after all, the usual, typical thing—the average. And you have seen for yourself that my uncle's family is not exceptional in these days. If you do not like them, you are at liberty to say so—I don't myself—but you must not say that they are abnormal... I daresay we have a laxer standard of sanity than you had in your day—I think that is what you are trying to say?"

"Yes," Guy almost shouted. And he was angry that John had put his meaning better than he could put it himself.

"Well," said John, "why not, if we can afford it? Possibly you had a laxer one than the eighteenth century... But I don't quite understand you. A moment ago you were angry with me for laughing at these people; now, you are abusing them yourself."

Guy walked on silently a moment, brooding. Then he cried out suddenly, in a surge of grief, and for a moment it seemed as if a voice not his own were speaking through him:

"Oh, what have you done with the world? What have you done with it? You have everything we ever wanted—everything to make you happy. I thought when I first came that all the nightmare was over. I thought you were all happy at last; and you are miserable—worse than miserable—so damnably hopeless that you clutch at every straw."

"I must contradict you," said John. "I am happy."

"Oh, God, yes, *you* are—you and your lot. That is the most detestable part of it. You build your happiness on the necks" (the old ranting phrase came back) "of millions of the miserable, just as it was in my day... *This* wasn't what we wanted. We thought— we thought—that, in these days, all mankind would be at one; that men would understand each other; that no one would lead a happy life while others were in misery. We thought that everything would be shared—pleasure and interest and knowledge, as much as clothes and food."

"Did you?" A wry smile was on John's lips for a second. "Emmanuel's dream! What," he added, "do you think we ought to do?"

Instead of answering, Guy burst out: "I would rather a thousand times be one of them than one of you!"

III

John, ignoring Guy's last exclamation, was explaining patiently. Most of the facts he stated Guy already knew. He could not have made it clear to John, nor did he clearly understand himself, why they did not touch the roots of his denunciation. And, all the more for this, the recital exasperated him.

"Unfortunately," John remarked, "it takes two to share interest and knowledge. You understand by this time that we are not an aristocratic, intellectual caste, who seize all the good things of life and keep them from everyone else? Everyone can learn who wishes; everyone who is fit can follow a scientific or artistic calling… I remember now, the idealists of your day thought that everyone would have an advanced education and become intellectual or artistic as soon as economic affairs were set straight. You worked so much in water-tight compartments in those days; your social writers and your psychologists seem hardly ever to have exchanged ideas."

"People could be taught," Guy muttered.

"You should try to teach a normal," John laughed. "Take Ena through a course of advanced chemistry, for instance. She would try—for you—but you would have to desist in sheer mercy… Are we too merciful for you? I remember that was the difficulty over the Euthanasia Palace.

"The experiment was tried, you know," he went on more seriously, "just because it was in the programme. At one time a university education was made compulsory for everyone. In a year or two it seemed probable that most of the population would spend its life at school trying to reach the necessary standard. In fact, the results were merely chaotic. The system was voted down almost unanimously at a General Election. It has not been tried again since. The people don't want to be educated. Why should they? They can live well without it. There is not now even the competitive stimulus which often led a man to acquire knowledge he did not really desire for itself."

Guy said, stammering a little: "They don't understand. If you cared about them… If you helped them—"

"How?" said John.

Again Guy was silent.

"Are we to go back to the old system?" John asked him. "When fear kept men at your standard of sanity? When they laboured and restrained themselves because they had to? Are we to destroy our wealth and abolish our organisation? Could you have abandoned the use of machinery—or democratic government? If we desired, we could not do it."

He said again a little later: "It is as Jesus said, 'The poor you have always with you.' We still have them, you see, after our manner. But it is no longer possible now to give them alms. They have all that we can give—that is, all that they can take. What more can we do?"

"And you are happy." Guy repeated the sullen accusation.

IV

John insisted on going into an inn to have breakfast, and in telephoning for some chemist's stuff to apply to the bruise on his cheek.

"I am going to be married to-morrow," he explained, with a smile, "so that I would prefer not to be discoloured."

The announcement caused a curious little interlude in the stormy conversation, while Guy, shaken momentarily out of his preoccupation, exclaimed and inquired in the old frank, friendly way. And for those few moments he actually felt frank and friendly, and John Wayland's young gallant beauty drew his heart again.

It was a casual word of John's that restarted the conflict—a conflict which, as perhaps they both knew by this time, was so fundamental that there could be only one ending to it.

"By the way, I think you are wrong in suggesting that all normals are unhappy. Consider my cousin Terry, for instance."

Guy laughed discordantly. There arose before him the figure of the big youth plunging around the treadmill of his hopeless, imaginary grievances against his father. He could see now, in his new enlightenment, that it was actually the sense of his inferiority, a perverted admiring love of his father, and the knowledge that he was a disappointment and an object of contempt to him, which underlay and poisoned all Terry's athletic triumphs. And if he had not had even that outlet...

"You don't even know!" he cried to John. "You don't even know!"

"Don't I? Well, you have lived in the house and I have not. No doubt he has his sore spot like the rest... Come now, Martin,

I'm sorry I renewed the subject. We have had enough of this. Be reasonable and accept facts as they are."

Guy realised that John had been very patient with him, and that his patience was now coming to an end. He felt glad and afraid. The last bout, the fiercest grip, he realised, was imminent. Mentally, he squared himself. With no clear idea of what it was that he was fighting, he knew beyond all reason that he must fight.

"I will not accept them," he cried in defiance, regardless now whether his words appeared ridiculous or not. "Not while there are men like you!"

v

Then the attack began. It began gently, casually, inexorably, as John's attacks would be certain to.

He was repeating quietly, as if to himself, the lines of Shelley:

> To suffer woes which hope thinks infinite,
> To forgive wrongs darker than death or night,
> To defy power that seems omnipotent,
> To love and bear, to hope till hope creates
> From its own wreck the thing it contemplates;
> Neither to change, nor falter, nor repent:
> This, like thy glory, Titan, is to be
> Good, great and joyous, beautiful and free:
> This is alone life, joy, empire and victory.

For Guy the passage was pregnant with old emotions. It had been a favourite with Marjorie Cannon. They had read *Prometheus*

Unbound together in the old time, which now seemed suddenly so innocent and idyllic, like the illusive memory of a passionate childhood. These lines had been spiritual inspiration to him in those days. Now they came off John Wayland's lips in light, compassionate mockery.

"That is what really explains you, Martin," said John. "I can see now how it is with you. I suppose the hypnotic suggestions disguised it before. You are the natural rebel, the Satanist—one of those unfortunates born with inverted instincts. Your necessity is to attack and to suffer. You may not know it, but, whatever your circumstances, you would seek out suffering. It was so in your own day, and it is so now. In no place nor time would you be at home. You are he who goes up and down upon the earth and to and fro in it."

To Guy it was as if he had become conscious during an operation and felt the surgeon's hand at his heart or in his entrails. The detachment, the absence of malignity in the attack, made it the more terrible. The truth of it invaded him like a corrosive acid. And yet he held to some reality, some ultimate certainty, behind his own writhing, dissected personality, something which John's words could not touch. He had to believe in this or be utterly destroyed. He could make no answer. All his will was strained to maintain his mental integrity against the assault.

"Curious," John continued musingly, "how that vein cuts across all strata of intellect."

Guy gasped out, maddened by the relaxation: "D— you! Stop your talking and your cataloguing. This is between you and me."

"Is it?" said John, glancing at him. "Between you and the nature of things, Martin. Between you and fact. Between you and me as their humble representative, perhaps."

Again one of those passionate irrelevancies swept Guy away.

"Humble! You humble! I should like to see you humbled. You had to kneel this morning, anyhow. Whatever you thought, you had to kneel with the rest." He thrust the words out viciously between grinding teeth.

"It seemed more prudent," said John a little wearily. "The present truth is," he went on, "that you are a Prometheus with nothing to fight against... That is a real tragedy! A Prometheus asked to suggest improvements and unable to find any suggestions... My poor Martin, you were better off in your own old century. Then there were real things, obvious to attack, and you could delude yourself with the belief that you had a real antagonist."

"Yes. We had hope then," Guy murmured.

John glanced at him. Guy saw an answer rise to his lips, a devastating answer, and fall suppressed. A terrible depression struck him, the utter humiliation of being at once understood and despised. However overwhelming the answer, it was worse that he was not thought worthy of it. John had become weary of him—the pain of that immediate human chagrin for a moment eclipsed everything else.

John said instead, stopping short on the road: "We shall get no farther, Martin. I only make it worse for you. Let me advise you to go back to my uncle, after all."

He had stopped beside the rank of aerocycles. Guy dully watched him mount and attach his power-box. He felt incapable of movement, although he was aware that some fatal misfortune was being consummated.

Then John was gone, with those flat trivial words. Guy felt suddenly weak, as if after a tremendous physical struggle. He staggered to a seat at the side of the road.

CHAPTER XI

GUY AND ENA

I

BESIDE THE INN PORCH, AS GUY ENTERED ON THE SAME afternoon, was sitting the gluttonous old man who had chosen him for the recipient of his table confidences. His swollen red face was bent over a newspaper, expanding the rolls of fat at the back of his neck. Guy caught sight of the headlines as he passed:

"EMMANUEL'S FAILURE"
"NOT LAST DAY, AFTER ALL"

They recalled to him for the instant the old racing headlines that he used once to see. He laughed without mirth. The old man glanced up and saw him.

"Hey, Martin," he exclaimed; "where have you been off all morning? So this Emmanuel is dead, and we have some chance of getting properly cooked dinners again. Did you see anything of it?"

Guy felt a sullen satisfaction that Emmanuel was dead. It was better than that he should have lived to be mauled physically and mentally by the doctors and sent off finally to a Euthanasia Palace.

"Yes, I saw it," he muttered reluctantly.

"Ha, ha! So you went? You were nicely taken in—" the old man guffawed. "And you have nearly missed something better."

One of his wrinkled eyelids drooped to a puffy cheek. "But I don't believe she's gone yet. I've been here all the time—on sentinel duty, as you might say. You take my advice, my son, and go up to your rooms just as quickly as you can. There's something pretty there for you."

The old man's leer was like an indecency. Guy hurried away from it, swearing under his breath. He would not wait to inquire what he meant. It was probably some mere stupid buffoonery.

He ran upstairs to his little sitting-room, and, as he opened the door, Ena, with bright, nervous, excited eyes, rose from the floor to meet him.

II

He stared at her stupidly for a moment.

Then she began to speak in the hard, quick tone of desperate embarrassment, her hands clasping and unclasping at her sides. "I found out where you were. I've been trying to find out ever since you went. I've watched John. I didn't believe you had gone right away. Someone I know saw you go in here last night and came and told me this morning. So I came here at once and waited for you… No one knows I've come."

Her presence exasperated Guy almost beyond endurance. In spite of his denials, he had known well enough that John's warning in regard to her on the day of their visit to the Euthanasia Palace was justified. And what was he to do with her now? The prospect of an emotional interview with her after the morning's experiences made him feel sick with disgust. He was almost in a mood for reckless cruelty.

He looked at her. Her eyes were swollen and her face was blotched with crying; her dark, frizzy hair was dishevelled. The shaky constraint of her speech and the intensity of her shining eyes played on his stretched nerves, so that he almost cried out at her to go away.

He restrained himself, but the effort put an edge into his voice as he asked: "Well, and what did you want me for?"

It was almost a relief that her precarious composure gave way at that.

"Oh, Guy, why did you go? It was cruel of you—cruel... Didn't you know it would nearly kill me?... I know I was dreadful that afternoon—like what you hate. But you might have given me another chance. I can't learn it all at once. How can I? You're too hard on me. I *was* trying. I *was*. I *was*."

"Trying? What on earth are you talking about? Oh, sit down, for God's sake."

"I will learn it. I will. If you'll only forgive me and help me... You only meant to punish me a little, didn't you?... You didn't know how it would hurt? I can do anything if you will only help me. If you'll just let me be with you. Then I shall remember, and begin to get more like you."

"Like me?" Guy's exclamation was half question and half groan.

"Oh, yes, if I only could. You're so different." Ena's words poured eagerly now. "Don't you see? I'd never seen anyone like you before. I didn't think there could be anyone like that. It was what happened on the mountain that day and the other times. You're not like the rest. You don't think girls are for nothing but to tease and make love to... I don't want you to make love to me—I don't really. I just want to be with you, as it was. I wouldn't be in the way… I'd be very careful. Don't you remember coming back from the mountain race. I was all right then, wasn't I?" Her eyes dwelt on him desperately, as if her salvation depended on the answer.

Guy stared at her. "Of course you were all right," he said slowly.

Ena seized the words out of his mouth triumphantly. "And you said I was a good pal. You did. And I was. I could be always. I could really. If you'd only give me a chance… I didn't understand before." She was struggling desperately after an unaccustomed lucidity. "None of *us* is like that. They want to make love all the time or get excited about something—not do things together and share and make fun, as we did that day… You don't like people to get excited. I wouldn't if I was with you. I'd be calm, madly calm, if you'd only give me a chance." A laugh that hurt him like a stab of pain half choked Guy.

"We could do all sorts of things," Ena went on urging. "Did you know there was a wild park in Africa?" She brought it out with a quick-drawn breath, studying his face as if it were an appeal that she had stored up to use when her need was greatest. "We could go there and camp out, and walk and get miles away where there'd be no aeroplanes or anything. They say there are a few lions left still. You could shoot them, if you liked… People did in your old times, didn't they? I'd have proper boots, I would really; and I'd learn to shoot, too. I'd look after you so nicely… And you would be nice to me, wouldn't you… Guy?"

She had knelt down beside him and her little brown hands were plucking at his arm in the eagerness of her appeal. She kept twisting her head so as to force him to meet her eyes, which sought his shamelessly like those of a child urgent for a treat.

Guy felt sick and shaken. He could only half follow her medley of absurdity. It was like the madness of this mad world that she should come to pester him just now with a passionate tirade about shooting lions and making love.

"I wish to God I knew what you were talking about," he burst out.

She shrank back, half-sitting on the carpet, with frightened eyes. A shudder passed through her and, with it, he saw her draw herself together, her features settle into a desperate determined calmness. It was the look of one who, utterly terrified, knows that he is fighting for his life and that his one poor remaining hope is to keep his head. Her childish face was white and pinched with the strain. It looked years older, and at the same time pathetically helpless.

"Of course you're right," she began to speak rapidly in a tense steady voice. "I haven't explained myself properly... You don't understand what you have done to me, but you have done it, and you must let me explain to you now... I've only understood since you came how dreadful it all was and how dreadful we all were... You see, I was brought up like that—all the ordinary people like me are. People like father and John won't have anything to do with us. They're kind to us, of course, but anyone can see that they don't think we are worth bothering about. And then, of course, we don't try any more as soon as we find that we aren't clever. We just get what we can and that seems to be all there is... Only then you came and you made everything seem different. You were so nice—like being children again, only nicer. Just friends. No one is real friends now, except intellectuals with each other. You know—you know... I used to be so jealous of them sometimes." Guy realised miserably that he was getting a genuine confession, one probably never formulated before even to herself. "They seemed to have so much fun together—real fun—not like us—we are as if—as if—we couldn't trust each other—I don't know why... But you seemed to like me—although I was so horrible—whenever I wasn't pretending. I pretend things too much, you know, about being a nun and all that. But I can stop it, if you will help me. I've felt ever so much more—more—a person, since it seemed as if you liked me... Oh, Guy, don't send me back. I couldn't go with my own sort of people again, after you. I couldn't."

Guy's face hardened. An anger based on panic sprang up in him at this suggestion of a responsibility for her future, which she was thrusting upon him. It was unfair, it was impossible, it was ridiculous of her to have based such fantastic hopes on his mere existence. He was not responsible for anything; he couldn't do anything. She had no business to appeal to him like this.

Ena saw the stiffening and her voice wavered.

"Don't send me back. I couldn't bear to go back. Oh, Guy, help me! I don't want—I don't want," her voice sank to a horrified whisper, "to grow like Mother... Don't you see? Why did you make me say it? Oh, let me stay with you... It's as if—as if—everything were clear and shining where you are... I could do anything for you. I could truly. I'd do anything you asked me. I'd kill myself if you wanted—no, you wouldn't like that... I mustn't say things like that—I'll learn not to, in time. You'll see... Oh, Guy, say something to me... You couldn't mean to leave me now after you've shown me... You must tell me what to do. There is no one but you."

She was half-sobbing against his knee again by this time.

To Guy it seemed as if the whole of her kind called and sobbed with her. He was oppressed by a hopeless, weary sorrow. It shamed as well as frightened him that, after all, as he was beginning to understand, it was not love so much as guidance that she was asking from him. He felt that he had done her wrong in his thoughts, insulted her undeservedly. Yet what she was demanding was even more unreasonable, more impossible. Guidance from him! He understood dimly that she had fashioned herself an ideal out of him, and now, with the ruthlessness of the worshipper, was demanding that he should play the part she had assigned to him. It was a ghastly farce. He looked inside his bankrupt soul and laughed.

Ena gave a little moaning scream. "Oh, don't laugh like that, Guy, don't. It breaks my heart. You are breaking it… If you are going to fail me, nothing will ever be any good again. Oh, if you aren't going to help me, why did you ever come? Why did you ever come?"

What could he say to her? Was there any hope for her and her kind? If there was, Guy knew that it was not he who could supply it. The challenge rang back in his own ears, his own challenge flung at John that morning—that they should try to help their "poor," after all; and he knew that he had neither the faith nor the courage for the attempt. He glanced down at Ena again and he could not even like her. He remembered that at one time he almost had, but that had been when it did not seem to matter. Now, clutching at him like this, she filled him with distaste and weariness. It oppressed him intolerably to know that there were millions more like her, uncontrolled tangles of emotion without a spice of wit or shrewdness. And yet she had been able to catch her one glimpse of beauty through him—the ghost of that old possibility of comradeship between ordinary people in the old world—a comradeship in which, ironically, he had actually shared so little. And she was coming to him, like iron to a magnet, to demand its realisation. She was pleading to him for something more essential than life—for a *raison d'être*. And what, in God's name, in all this horrible universe, was he to say to her?

He hoped that she would take his silence for an answer, but she would not. She hung about his knees, moaning, now and then looking agonisingly up at him.

"Look here, Ena," he said at last, weakly. "I'm very tired—"

She seized on the respite eagerly. "Oh, oh, I'm sorry. I'm bothering you when you're tired. I'll go… You'll let me come again sometime…? Or you'll come back to us?" The eagerness in her voice nearly broke him down. "Terry isn't there—it's very quiet," she twisted her terror-stricken features into a ghastly smile.

Guy groaned inwardly. He understood that he could expect no help towards decisiveness from her. And he felt that he must not leave the miserable business hanging—to have her constantly turning up with her ridiculous demands.

"I shan't come back to you, Ena," he said. "And I don't want you here. You have made a mistake. I can't do anything for you in the way you want. You had better go back to your own sort of people and stay there."

The hard, brutal voice seemed to be coming without his conscious volition. It was like this, he supposed, that crimes were committed. Some automatic mechanism looked after the action, while one stood aside and watched impassively.

Ena was quite still and silent for a second. He had got up roughly, as he spoke, thrusting back his chair, so that she was left kneeling on the carpet. Then her arms went up above her head, as if warding off a blow.

"No, no, no," she said. "No, no."

It was like the terrible, naïve, protesting cry of a child being brutally beaten. "No, no, no."

Overtaken by nausea, Guy groped his way to the door. Ena had dropped forward and lay full length, her head buried in her arms. He pushed blindly at the door and went out.

CHAPTER XII

SUCH THINGS AS DREAMS

I

THAT NIGHT GUY DREAMT LONG AND VIVIDLY THAT HE was back in the twentieth century. He had often returned in sleep to the old life, re-enacting scenes in which he had played a part, calling up forgotten personalities, embroidering old incidents with a confusion of fresh variations. But to-night it was none of the things specifically connected with his own life that came back to him out of the past. It was a more generalised experience, the life of the London streets which he had passed through unnoticing a thousand times. All the details which had made the background of existence in those old days came thronging through his brain, like actors stepping up to the footlights, starting one after another into full significance.

It was the London of the evening hours in which he was wandering—such another chill, drizzling evening as that on which he had received Marjorie Cannon's final letter. It seemed to him at times that he had an appointment to keep, that he was to meet someone at some place before the night was over, and that meanwhile he travelled to and fro incessantly about the great city on devious routes to his rendezvous, a lost unit among the thronging people, impersonal as a wandering ghost.

As he went, certain things, impressions, started vividly out of the crowd from time to time as if picked out by spotlight, to vanish again the next moment into blackness.

There was the lighted interior of the 'bus in which he travelled through shadowy surburban streets towards the glare of the city—a 'bus of the old type in which the passengers sat facing one another. Opposite to him a row of white impassive faces stood out against the rain-sprinkled panes behind them, across which passed from time to time the shining track of street lamps and of lighted shops. His eye ran along from face to face. That of the man over against him had broad, coarse, protuberant features of the kind associated with caricatures of butchers. The sweat-drops stood out on it against the greasy skin. He was stout and somewhat uncleanly, and it was noticeable that the neatly threadbare girl next to him, who looked pale and pinched like a clerk or school teacher out of work, shrank away from him slightly into the corner. The young man on the other side of him had the lower part of his thin face cut off from sight by a newspaper, on which Guy read the large black headline: "Ex-Officer's Suicide." Beyond him again was a woman nursing a small, quiet baby in a shawl. She was languid and unhealthy-looking, her worn face was relaxed and her eyes half-closed, as if the journey in the jolting 'bus were a respite to her.

The 'bus stopped, and a man who had been sitting next to Guy got out. A little group was waiting near the step to climb in. Guy saw that they were hanging back while the conductor assisted a woman up the step and into the interior. He wondered why they were not pushing and struggling to get on as usual. Then he saw that it was one of those odd, decrepit females who were part of the jetsam of the London life of those days. She had an elderly, wrinkled, leaden-hued face framed by straggling wisps of grey hair under a big hat with sweeping feathers, which was twisted on one side and out of shape. Her body showed distorted in a long, trailing skirt and a pretentious tailor-made coat belonging to another suit. Around her neck hung a dirty feather boa. As she hobbled laboriously into the 'bus, impelled by the impassive conductor, the passengers glanced at her furtively in an involuntary, shocked interest. She took the vacant seat beside Guy, who instinctively drew himself away from the horror of her neighbourhood. But the creature, whom it was impossible to regard as human, as if with a goblin-like malice, edged herself close to him again. One claw-like hand with black-rimmed nails rested against his overcoat. In an access of repulsion, he sprang up, tugged violently at the cord, and pushed his way to the door.

II

Without consciousness of transition he was leaving Charing Cross Station. And out of the rain and half-darkness appeared a face. It was that of a man who offered him matches as he stepped out of the courtyard into the teeming road. It stood out clear of its surroundings, an isolated human face—a cowed, imploring wistfulness in its deep-set eyes—not the face of a man offering to trade in something that might conceivably be wanted; it was the face of one asking for charity, for anything, for some sort of recognition at any price, a face sick and hopeless with disappointment.

Guy, carried on the current of the old habit, shook his head as he passed him. A voice seemed to be repeating in his brain words that he must have heard more than once. "One must not give to people in the streets." It made a sort of refrain as he stepped along the pavement. And, as he went, his humanity shrank insulted within him at the memory of that expression. He felt his own shoulders rounding, his own gait become the slinking of a beaten dog.

III

Again, he was hurrying along the Euston Road, trying to reach his rendezvous. Something horrible—he did not clearly know what—would happen if he did not arrive in time. The damp, slippery pavements, gleaming here and there in the electric lamps, hindered him, and people continually got in his way. He crossed to the quieter south side in order to progress more quickly, and entered a dark patch where the trees from a railed-in square overhung the pavement. And as he pressed forward, a figure moved swiftly out of the shadows, intercepting him.

"In a hurry, aren't you?" He was not sure that she spoke, but the words echoed in his brain, as he looked down at her slight figure and upturned face. He was even aware of a certain timidity which quavered under their professional impudence, forcing him to realise that the speaker was a novice at her trade. She had fastened her hands on to his arm and was bending backwards looking up at him. In the dim light he could just make out a rounded young face, thickly plastered with rouge and powder. The eyes were full, and fuzzy dark hair was pushed out from under the jaunty little hat. The thought cropped up automatically from his old store of associations that she ought to be in Piccadilly; she was not old enough yet to be relegated to this part.

It seemed to him that he must have seen her somewhere before, but he could not spare time to consider now. He would be late for his appointment. He disengaged himself silently, with as little roughness as possible, and the girl shrank back into the shadows. She did not make the second attempt that a practised hand would certainly not have omitted.

IV

It seemed that the strange quest persisted through many hours and many places. Now he was tramping through gas-lighted back streets where children shrieked and sombre crowds pressed along the wet pavements; now he was among the blazing light-signs of the West End, dodging the whirring taxis which disgorged warm, brilliant women, and men in evening dress before the theatre entrances. And always, as he tried to progress to this rendezvous on which it seemed that everything depended, he was hampered, dragged at, kept back, turned aside by a thousand and one mischances. The person with whom he was to keep the rendezvous varied; sometimes it was Marjorie Cannon, sometimes Burrows from the bank on a business matter, sometimes, curiously, his mother. But, more often, it was some other vague person whom he knew, but for whom he had no name.

At one time it seemed that it was the supper hour, and that it was essential that he should have a meal before he kept the appointment, although he was not conscious of hunger. And, with the thought, he was sitting with dishes before him in a small, dimly lighted restaurant with white-clothed tables and a stone floor. Except for a few scattered diners and a waiter who hovered and disappeared, the room was prevailingly shadowy and silent.

In the corner behind him two men were sitting over their meal. He could not see them, and they were out of earshot, but their conversation came to him as if by a direct intuition. It began with the sense of an atmosphere of spurious heartiness rising from the corner like an emanation. In the heart of it he was conscious of the larger man talking.

"My dear chap, I'll do whatever I can for you, you may be sure." There was an unctuous rounding of the words and a lingering enjoyment in them.

"I know you will, Jack." The reply was a quick, half-shamed whisper. This man was anxious not to be overheard. "You don't know how I hate asking you—"

"But, my dear fellow, why?" The big man overwhelmed him resoundingly. "Haven't we been friends—let me see—more than twenty years now? As I say, I'll be delighted to do anything I can. Of course, it's a bad time—"

"I know."

"There isn't anything just at present, I'm afraid, but there might be, of course... Well, well, well, to think of Hinckson & Merivale going! And you were always so proud of their credit, old man. Ha, ha, ha! That's one on you. Pity you didn't come out when I advised you to years ago."

"I don't remember that"; there was a shade of asperity now in the meekness of the other voice.

"Don't you?" The atmosphere of heartiness became a shade less strong. "Oh, come now. I've always said that firm would come to a bad end; as far back as the rubber boom I said it. You must remember that?"

The other rejoined anxiously, propitiatingly: "Well, perhaps you did, Jack. I've been so worried lately, I'm forgetting things. But now about this new berth—" The sentence quavered and sank.

"Here, steady, not so fast. You mustn't think it's all ready for you to drop into... Of course, I'll do what I can... Would you be prepared to take an undermanager's or secretary's post under me, if a vacancy could be made?"

"It isn't what I've been used to, Jack," said the other quiveringly, after a short pause. "We couldn't live as we have. We should have to move into a smaller house. My wife—"

"Now, Bob, take it right from me at the beginning. That sort of talk is no good, no good at all. One has to face facts. You've come a bad cropper, and you mustn't expect to begin again exactly where you left off. All your friends will be only too anxious to help you; but if you're going to take that line—"

"No, no, Jack; of course I understand. It can't be the same thing. I'll be glad of anything you can get me... You must make allowances... One has to get accustomed—"

"Of course I will, old man. And damned hard luck it is, too! But there you are... Well, I'll consult old Phelps. It won't be easy, but we might manage to make some re-arrangements."

"I'll be eternally grateful if you will, Jack. You don't know what it is to be a family man and to feel—"

"Now, now, now, that's all right, that's all right!"

The heartiness seemed to swell and spread until it filled the room.

V

For a second the room about Guy dissolved and he was again before Charing Cross Station re-enacting the little scene with the match-seller. As from outside he saw himself turning away with the careless gesture of denial and the man's cowed, beseeching eyes, which seemed to concentrate in their depths all the misery and disappointment of humanity in its lot.

And with that, once again, automatically, the words repeated themselves:

"One must not give to people in the streets."

Then that also vanished and he was back again in the little restaurant. It seemed to be darker now. Several lights had evidently been turned out. The two men in the corner had gone and there were only one or two diners left sitting quietly apart and scattered. Opposite to Guy a young man sat at a table with a half-empty plate pushed back and a cup of coffee before him. Guy had not noticed him before, but his eyes were drawn to him now. He had a thin, dark face, very pale, and he was in constant nervous movement. Guy knew, as he looked, with instinctive human recognition of the unnatural, that the other was the victim of some evil obsession. His skin was the colour of lead and the shadows about his eyes were thick, black smudges. The muscles about his lips and eyes twitched incessantly; he clasped and unclasped his hands, lifted them on and off the table, took out a cigarette and abandoned it. His dark, restless eyes gleamed like black pools. From time to time he made a half-suppressed exclamation, and would begin to rise from his chair, only to sink back, glancing around him suspiciously.

Not mad yet, but near it, Guy reflected. Probably a drug-taker. He determined to keep quiet and not attract his attention. He tried to persuade himself that he was merely prudent, but he was actually afraid of the young man, and dared not get up to go about his urgent business while the other was there.

It seemed to him as if he sat watching interminably. It was borne in upon him that the other man had some ghastly, insane decision to make, that he was sitting there trying in his disordered mind to find the resolution for some act of horror. At times he spoke almost above his breath, evidently holding some strange debate with himself, but Guy could never catch the words.

Suddenly, a clock just at hand began to strike, and, immediately, as if released by the outside stimulus, the young man sprang to his feet with a crackling laugh and made a dart towards the door. As he went, staggering awkwardly, he caught the edge of the table just beside Guy, and, for a second, as he was pulled round, his eyes looked into Guy's. A smile, the remnant of the mad laugh, lingered there. Then he was gone.

John! It was John! Guy cried out, as the place whirled around him. It was John, gone to meet some atrocious necessity. And in the same moment, he knew that he had missed his appointment, that he had failed, that it was too late.

Suddenly, through his anguish, he realised that he was dreaming and willed to wake.

He came up slowly through swirling darkness. For an instant, which might have been an eternity, there floated again beside him the white-swathed image of the Sufferer with whom he had once watched through the passage of the centuries. Then he opened his eyes again upon the walls of his riverside bedroom whitening in the approaching dawn.

VI

Guy lay on his side and looked out. He could see through the wide-opened shutters of his room the beautiful twenty-second century landscape of trees and meadows and half-hidden houses. It came out gradually, like a developing photograph, in the dawn. The river, too close at hand to be seen, he heard faintly, a rustling background of sound to the twittering of the birds. Still and lovely and lifeless the country lay, until the tiny graceful shape of an aeroplane danced momentarily across the lightening sky and disappeared again.

Guy gazed. He sighed and moved a little on the bed, feeling the pliancy of his young limbs. His brain was heavy with terrible knowledge.

A glow appeared in the Eastern sky, spread slowly, and intensified at its centre. As on the day before when Emmanuel had gathered his followers to greet it, Guy watched the sun rise yet once more upon the world of men.

A NOTE FROM THE PUBLISHER

It has been our pleasure to rediscover this pioneering, yet largely forgotten work of science fiction by this unjustly neglected writer. Our thanks go to Mike Ashley for his suggestion to consider *The Question Mark* for the British Library Science Fiction Classics series, and to the Estate for their cooperation and enthusiasm in bringing Muriel Jaeger's imaginative novel back to the printed page. Jaeger is a fascinating figure, and we encourage those interested to seek out the texts in the Further Reading section of Dr Moulton's introduction for more information.

We hope you, too, have enjoyed exploring this speculative picture of the twenty-second century, and, should you be hungry for more classic science fiction, we have a number of short story anthologies and novels currently available from British Library Publishing.

SHORT STORY ANTHOLOGIES
EDITED BY MIKE ASHLEY

Lost Mars:
The Golden Age of the Red Planet

Moonrise:
The Golden Age of Lunar Adventures

Menace of the Machine:
The Rise of AI in Classic Science Fiction

The End of the World
and Other Catastrophes

Menace of the Monster:
Classic Tales of Creatures from Beyond

Beyond Time:
Classic Tales of Time Unwound

CLASSIC SCIENCE
FICTION NOVELS

By William F Temple

Shoot at the Moon
Four-Sided Triangle

By Charles Eric Maine

The Tide Went Out
The Darkest of Nights

By Ian Macpherson

Wild Harbour

We welcome any suggestions, corrections or feedback you may have, and will aim to respond to all items addressed to the following:

The Editor (Science Fiction Classics)
British Library Publishing
The British Library
96 Euston Road
London, NW1 2DB

We also welcome enquiries through our Twitter account, @BL_Publishing.

CLASSIC LITERARY SCIENCE FICTION
BY IAN MACPHERSON

15 May 1944 – This morning I said to Terry,
'I thought I heard guns through the night.'
'Were you awake too?' she asked.

Something has happened in Europe. Fearing the approach of war to Britain, Terry and Hugh retreat from their home to the remote highlands of Scotland, prepared to live a simple existence together whilst the fighting resolves itself far away.

Encouraged by Terry, Hugh begins a journal to note down the highs and lows of this return to nature, and to process their concerns of the oncoming danger. But as the sound of guns by night grow louder, the grim prospect of encroaching war threatens to invade their cherished isolation and demolish any hope of future peace.

Macpherson's speculative novel of future war was first published in 1936, just 3 years before the outbreak of the Second World War in Europe.